SNARE OF THE FOWLER

SNARE OF THE FOWLER

TOM TAYLOR

MOODY PRESS
CHICAGO

© 1977 by
THE MOODY BIBLE INSTITUTE
OF CHICAGO

All rights reserved

Library of Congress Cataloging in Publication Data
Taylor, Tom, 1944-
  Snare of the fowler.

  I. Title.
PZ4.T24645Sn   [PS3570.A956]   813'.5'4   77-22322
ISBN 0-8024-8104-3

Printed in the United States of America

Contents

CHAPTER   PAGE

    Preface 7
1. All Is Not Well in the Afternoon Sky ... 9
2. The Joy and the Curse 23
3. Satan Is Not Easily Defeated at Asoe ... 42
4. For Want of a Nail 62
5. Of the Here and Hereafter 77
6. *La Amaba Hasta Que Murio* 99
7. In the Clouds Lies Eternity 112
8. Home Before Dark 129
9. As the Stars Forever 144

I will say of the Lord, He is my refuge and my fortress: my God; in Him will I trust. Surely he shall deliver thee from the snare of the fowler. . .
Psalm 91:2-3

Preface

This story had its conception in the experiences of various missionaries serving in many places around the world whom I have been privileged to know—most of them through the mission support program of my home church, Shenandoah Baptist, of Roanoke, Virginia. Most of the story's characters are patterned after these missionaries currently serving in many locations around the world. I want to give special thanks to Mr. Norman Keefe, of New Tribes Mission, who is currently working with the Moro Indians of Paraguay, South America. His willingness to share his experience and knowledge was invaluable in creating the fictional Edigo Indians of this story, which have been patterned largely after the Moro Indians of Paraguay.

I would also like to thank the several pilots of Jungle Aviation and Radio Service (JAARS) who graciously shared their advice and experiences with me. I want to emphasize that of the missionary pilots I interviewed or flew with, none suffered from the spiritual malaise encountered by the pilot in this story. That, happily, is a product of my writer's imagination only.

This story, of a particularly vicious skirmish in the conflict of the ages, depicts the tragic results when Christians depart from the will of their Lord and how God can triumph even through the mistakes of his servants. It is hoped this story will illuminate a truth that you may not have previously considered: a life dedicated to Christ is a life of adventure in its most rewarding sense.

1

All Is Not Well in the Afternoon Sky

The wilderness of the Gran Chaco, the gnarled, wind-stunted *quinee pede* trees, "Old Lady's Skin," as the Moro Indians call them, thick and entangled with vines, lay beneath an aging afternoon sun. High over it drifted the sunlit speck of a light plane droning through the endless sky. For missionary pilot Paul Graham, alone with the sky and wind, the engine's droning was security; its noise and vibration a blanket enfolding him against the harsh land below. He did not think about it just so, for at the time he was too busy. In the afternoon air currents, his single-engine DeVoss B was bouncing like a cork, and his feet danced on the rudder pedals in an effort to keep the gyrocompass steady. *That's it. Keep the little white 30 in the compass window. Three hundred degrees north-northwest.* That was the magic number that would take him to Asoe, main village of the Edigo Indians. It would take him there, that is, if he had guessed the wind correctly. He would soon know.

Ordinarily the young, sandy-haired pilot was at home in the air. Soft-spoken and quiet, he was a loner but an adventurer whose spirit knew a kinship with the wind so playfully tossing his ship. But this flight had not been pleasant; he shifted uneasily in his seat and, for the tenth time, listened warily to the faultless engine. Something was wrong, yes, but not with the engine—something besides the heat and rough air, too. He did not believe in premonition, yet a vague uneasiness from far back in his mind warned him that all was not well in the afternoon sky. More annoying than that, he could not put his finger on just what it was. Perhaps, his subconscious suggested cruelly, it was because the plane he was flying had so recently killed a human being partly because of Paul's own stupidity. No! No, that was absolutely not the reason. Would it ever leave him alone?

His troubled thoughts were interrupted as, about five miles ahead, the hazy outlines of a small hill emerged through the yellow sun glare. This should be Roundtop, the small knoll penciled on his aerial chart as one of the few landmarks available in the area. Soon he distinguished around the knoll's base a dry creekbed, which, in the rainy season, was a tributary of the Rio Paraguai, far to the east. *OK. Got it made.* This was Roundtop, all right. He now knew that the Village and its six-hundred-foot grass airstrip lay only fifteen miles westward on a track of 280 degrees. Thus Paul found his way through an area lacking directional radio stations or even good landmarks. Here, northwest toward the Bolivian border, the Chaco was a faceless blend of scrub jungle and open grassland. How uncanny that Paul could fly over it so many times, and still every square mile looked just like the one before it! It was a navigator's nightmare.

Even though he was sure of his location now, the haunting malaise clung to the back of his mind like a lizard in the dark. He irritably grasped the microphone for his routine position call. *"Eighty-six Zulu* calling Colonia base. Over."

From two hundred miles south at Interior Evangelism headquarters in Colonia, the answer finally came, as a husky voice rumbled over the speaker. "This is Colonia base, Paulo. Over."

A tight smile flickered on Paul's full lips. His friend Alfredo Savillas spoke Guarani by preference; and his radio Spanish always struck Paul as somewhat comical. He was glad to hear it; glad the radio was functioning, for lately it had been giving trouble; glad for another human voice to assure him he was still part of the earth. "Alfredo," he answered. "Hasn't Nancy come in yet? Over."

"She still must be sleeping, Paulo. The whole of the night she has been awake, tending Ijomejene at the clinic. Over."

"Very well. All right. I'm fifteen miles from Asoe on 280 degrees right now, and I'm going in to pick up the Indian. How about the gasoline at Bahia? Over."

"I have been calling Bahia," Alfredo said, "but I cannot hear an answer. Perhaps no one is tending the radio just now. But I will keep trying. How much fuel have you now, Paulo? Over."

"I'm down to about twelve gallons in each wing. That should be enough for the return trip to Colonia, but—" Paul, typically, left the sentence unfinished. The wise pilot doesn't allow his fuel supply to drain too low over an area like this, little changed since the Spanish explorer Ayolas disappeared in its depths centuries before.

Savillas, also a pilot, understood. "Very well, Paulo. Perhaps I can learn if there is any fuel available at Bahia before you leave Asoe. Also I should tell you there are many thunderclouds coming up, and the sky is dark south of here. Puerto Sastre says it appears to be a front, but we are unsure of its movement. Over."

Paul bit his lip. *Great!* That was all he needed to really foul things up: being forced to detour around storms on the trip back, consuming even more of his marginal fuel. "Thanks for that, Alfredo," he said finally. "Keep after Bahia for me, and I'll call you as soon as I'm airborne from Asoe. If Bahia has any gas on hand, I'll detour over there for sure. Keep an eye on the weather there too." The last instruction was needless, Paul knew, and he felt a little foolish for having said it. Savilla's would watch the weather and shadow him with radioed advice like a mother hen.

They signed off then. The engine rumble softened as Paul throttled back to let the plane bleed off altitude and slowly slide down from the sky during these last ten miles. But even with slower airspeed, his plane still bucked and rolled. With the afternoon air this turbulent, it was not surprising that thunderstorms were building somewhere.

His mind drifted again to the vague alarm bell ringing in his subconscious. "OK, Graham," he muttered to himself, "what is it?" He had to pinpoint whatever was causing this subtle twisting of his entrails, for in the air, forgetting something can kill you. The fact that this flight was for a medical emergency could not account for his tension. He had flown more critically ill patients than he could remember, and there was no reason this Indian whom he was soon to pick up should bother him any more than the others. Maybe it was because his fuel was getting uncomfortably low for the two hundred-mile trip back. No, it was not that, either. The fuel problem was tangible and easily seen; whatever was bothering him was not.

Oh blast this flight anyway! he thought in exasperation. It had started out all wrong. He would be fat with fuel right now except that yesterday evening the propeller seals had sprung a leak and prevented him from reaching his home base and fuel.

He had been returning to Colonia through an evening sky afloat with fat, cumulus jellyfish trailing their tentacles of rain, when telltale drops of oil began flecking the windshield. The nearest airstrip was the military outpost of Fortin Coronel Francisco Varisca, so reluctantly he radioed Nancy that he would be spending the night there. The runway at Varisca was clay, recently drenched by a passing shower, and Paul slithered wildly to a stop through the wisps of rising steam. *And why did the Baptiste pilot remain so long in his cockpit?* they probably wondered. They did not guess that it was to let his shaking subside. The involuntary trembling of his hands and knees had become all to common recently, especially since the accident of two months ago when his carelessness had killed—

The dapper, young *subteniente* at Varisca offered Paul a meal and a bunk for the evening. His small fort, he said proudly, was quite luxurious in comparison with most isolated posts, and a brick mess hall complete with antiseptic tile floor justified the officer's pride. Before the meal, Paul rose to introduce himself to the sixty gathered soldiers, speaking to them in Spanish, for he was not yet fluent in the ancient Indian language Guarani, which was preferred by most men there. Paraguay is one of the few countries where the conquering Spanish, rather than slaughtering the native Indians, intermarried with them, and thus the two languages flourish side by side. His hosts understood well enough, however, as he explained how leaking propeller seals had forced this unscheduled stop. "And I want to thank you, first, for having a runway located so conveniently for me—"

They laughed.

"And then for the food and a place to sleep. Certainly this is superior to a night in the forest, listening to the jaguar."

Then, because he was a "man of God," at the subteniente's request, he awkwardly blessed the food, and they ate.

There was something Paul liked about this officer. Perhaps it was that he ate with the enlisted men, and though he was on a first-name basis with each of them, there seemed to be no question of his command or of their respect for him. His, then, was genuine authority, needing no crutch of formality or ritual. Probably this was his first command, and Paul wondered if, when the subteniente rose through officer ranks, he would remain as amiable as now. Probably he would. If his first command did not go to his head, it was unlikely that future promotions would affect him either. The officer, Paul decided, was a good man.

As they ate, talk of the recent Montonero guerrilla raid on Formosa worked its way into the conversation.* It was an uncomfortable topic, because Formosa is close by the Argentine border with Paraguay.

"I understand that the governor escaped unharmed," Paul said.

"Yes, he slipped out of their hands during the confusion at the air terminal. *Valgame dios!* The man has courage and good fortune!" The subteniente, unlike the quiet Paul Graham, spoke with intensity, as though at any moment he would spring to the table top to deliver an oration. "But Senor Graham, I tell you what feature of this raid most impresses me. The discipline, the presence of mind of these guerrillas after their initial plan failed, and they are not trained soldiers. For instance, their intended target was the infantry garrison at Formosa, was it not?"

"I suppose for the weapons and ammunition," Paul offered.

"Yes. Fortunately, they were defeated there, and about fifteen of them were killed. But the thirty still left retained their wits. They fight their way to the airport, take the federal governor prisoner at the terminal, and commandeer a jet,—"

"A Boeing 737 wasn't it?" Paul asked quietly.

---

*This attack occurred on Formosa, an Argentine provincial capital, in October 1975, and was reported by the Telam News Agency and the Associated Press in Buenos Aires.

He had heard of the *Aerolineas Argentinas* flight hijacked by the Montoneros between Buenos Aires and Corrientes and diverted to Formosa. "So I agree with you, senor; they were disciplined and coordinated as well."

The subteniente sighed. "The world is becoming a turbulent place, my friend. Why is it that men will form themselves into tightly disciplined groups such as this? Risk their lives?"

Paul didn't know if his host really wanted an answer. "A desire for adventure?" he said. "Perhaps the Robin Hood complex."

That analogy was lost on the Paraguayan, and a trace of a frown flicked across his face. "What of the desperation of a stomach aching with hunger? And the knowledge that no matter how diligently you work, there will only be more of the same?"

"In other words, if most people were content with their lives, leftist promises would have little appeal to them?"

"Correct." The officer smiled. "It is a problem that we must recognize, that we must face. What can we offer these people as an alternative? The United States is traditional leader of the free nations. What can the United States offer to people who will grasp any promise of a better life, no matter how illusory? What can the United States offer? Capitalism?"

Paul felt a rising discomfort. Was the subteniente only making conversation, asking a genuine question, or was he perhaps issuing a challenge? Paul did not enjoy debates. He appeared younger than his twenty-eight years, with a sunburned face crinkling into crow's-feet around his grinning eyes. Until recently he was more at ease peering over the nose of an airplane than addressing a congregation or debating a friend. Thus his colleagues were usually surprised to find in him a philosophical turn of mind, to find that his opinions were well formed, though usually he was reluctant to voice them.

"Capitalism, senor?" he said in stilted Spanish. "I don't know. The advantage of capitalism is that individuals own the wealth of a country rather than the government. So it serves as a guarantee of freedom at least from excessive government power. Of course, capitalism without Christian principles can be oppressive as well as any other system. But I can tell you this, friend. Any system, any system at all is better than the extreme left: Communism. That system uses brute force to deny the existence of a man's spirit and soul. That is the horror of it. Most dictators enslave the body. Communism tries to enslave every part of you—your body, soul, spirit, will, imagination."

"Very good, and I agree. But can you convince someone of this when his stomach is empty?"

Paul conceded. "Probably no, you couldn't."

"What then can the United States offer?"

Paul sighed, for his host was pushing inexorably toward a painful cul-de-sac. "You know I can't speak for the United States or what it can offer," he said. "But I can tell you my own opinion—that the only real alternative to slavery is to convince men of the truth that their souls are immortal; that to find God and do his will is the only path to any real happiness. If a man misses this, he has missed the reason he was created. And a man who believes this with his heart will never be a slave to any system."

The subteniente was mildly surprised at this turn in the conversation. Yet Paul's words smacked of the impractical, and the officer was disturbed as well by a lack of conviction in the pilot's voice. "Very well, then," he said. "And how is one to find God, or know what is his will, Senor Graham?"

Paul hesitated. *Tell him, the man is searching! Tell him Jesus said: "I am the way, the truth, and the life: no man cometh to the Father, but by me."* [†] *Tell him that surrender to Jesus Christ will free his soul from sin, which is the ultimate slavery in this world!* But Paul Graham did not speak of Christ. How could he speak of a relationship to Jesus Christ when he was no longer sure of his own? How could he say that faith in Christ would solve the world's problems when it was not solving his?

The officer waited for a moment and smiled.

[†]John 14:6.

"Perhaps I have asked the impossible question, eh?" And in a moment the conversation turned, sadly, to the trivial and meaningless. This confirmed the subteniente's view of churchmen. Ah, their words sounded nice enough but paled to nothing in the glare of reality, on the level where men like himself must live. And he was disappointed. Somehow he had hoped for something more concrete from this Christian pilot. Why, he wondered, did Paul perform a hazardous task for God, when seemingly he could not describe the way to know Him?

In the morning, Paul, a licensed aircraft mechanic as well as pilot, had repaired the Fairingdale propeller hub, replacing the seals from a kit of spare parts he carried routinely, for his fifteen-year-old DeVoss was getting pretty tired at this stage of the game. And that afternoon he departed Coronel Varisca, glad for the hospitality but glad as well to be free of that boredom and tension that haunts military bases universally. And he was also glad to be rid of that subteniente and his penetrating questions.

It was then that the shortwave had crackled alive with the gravelly voice of Ed Fucelli, Interior Evangelism's missionary to the Edigo Indians at Asoe. "One of Inacarai's sons has been lanced in the chest, Paul." he radioed. "The Edigo Sota have got their war chants going; if he dies we're going to have some real trouble out here. How soon can you get here and pick him up? Over."

"Will he need a doctor soon?" Paul queried.

"He'll need a surgeon, Paul. It's a barbed lance point in his chest. You will need to fly him to the clinic at Colonia or Filadelfia. Over."

Irritation flickered immediately as Paul mentally calculated the trip out to Asoe and then back to Colonia: roughly two and a half hours of flying time, depending on the wind, and that was almost exactly the duration of the fuel supply in his tanks. "Brother!" he muttered. *Why must the decisions always be so close? Always in that gray area–* "Look, Ed, I've got to go back to Colonia and gas up before I can come out there. And it'll be dark in about four hours. Can your patient wait until tomorrow morning? Over."

The radio was silent for a few minutes as Fucelli apparently conferred with his wife, a nurse. His voice, when he transmitted again, was tired and drained. "Paul, he won't last the night. Marilyn says his chest cavity is filling with blood; she doesn't believe he can live that long without surgery. Over."

And so it was that Paul Graham found himself descending toward Asoe that strange afternoon with his fuel growing too low for comfort and with a curious fear he could neither explain nor ignore. Soon he must begin the delicate task of getting his plane down and stopped on the six-hundred-foot grass airstrip; and then, he thought gratefully, there would be no more time for this introspective nonsense. For that, at least, he was glad. For lately Paul Graham was frightened of where his thoughts would lead him.

2

The Joy and the Curse

The disintegration of a man's faith, and with it his courage, is usually a gradual process. Not so for Paul Graham. He could remember the very night it had begun for him, a night two weeks after the accident, a spring September evening with the Assassin's Wind blowing hot and dry, laden with the warm sweetness of orange blossoms. Beside the small airfield at Colonia stood the brick house, regional headquarters for Interior Evangelism Mission in Paraguay. Paul remembered the fragrant wind puffing through closed shutters to tease the kerosene lamp flames. The wood-burning power plant in Colonia was out of order again, and Dr. Pearson, regional director for the mission, was saving their diesel generator to power the shortwave the next day. It was unfortunate, for he was growing slowly blind from an eye disease he had contracted in Equador. He already had to peer through thick glasses with an inset lens for reading.

Now the saintly old gentleman and his wife

smiled at their two young dinner guests, Paul and Nancy Graham, seated in wicker chairs around the laminated table. The dinner party could have been a happy one. But Paul remembered a gloom so thick that, with the heat from the lamp, it seemed likely to stifle his breathing; and Nancy, his pug-nosed little wife, was crying.

"I don't know," she sobbed. "It's awful. I can't love anybody—I can't love God or even Paul anymore!"

Paul bit his lip. This was getting personal. But then, it was supposed to be a counseling session, was it not? It was combined with dinner, of course, but the *soo-yosopy* and iced *yerba mate* were tasteless in his dry mouth.

"Nancy," Dr. Pearson said gently, "I've known many Christians who've suffered the loss of a child. Most of them have emerged from the experience with their faith stronger, their love for the Lord more vibrant than before."

"Why isn't it working for me, then?" Her harsh sob was almost a shout of despair.

"I believe we should talk out your feelings, Nancy. And we'll explore God's Word together and find out why it isn't 'working,' as you say. I really believe this is only a temporary reaction."

Paul fervently hoped it was only temporary. But he realized, too, that the death of their four-year-old son was doubly tragic because he and Nancy must both share the blame for it. And guilt added to grief becomes a burden twice as great.

He taxied to the front of the hangar at Colonia and waved to Nancy and little Eddy as they stood waiting, smiling in the setting sun. Nearly exhausted from a hard day, he pulled the carburetor mixture to full lean and settled back to wait the usual few seconds it would take for the engine to die. From the corner of his eye he saw Eddy running toward the plane. Why didn't Paul think to cut the magneto switch at that very second, so the propeller may have stopped in time? Why did he just sit in frozen shock as the little redhead vanished from his sight beneath the cowl and that horrible shudder ran through the plane? It was too late then, of course, and he fell from the cockpit door and wretched violently as he saw on the ground the bloody heap that was once his son.

People, even little children, die in the most ridiculous ways. Throughout those nightmarish days Paul and Nancy were surrounded by the strengthening presence of their missionary friends. And yet it seemed that a muted horror hung over all present. Eddy's death had been so sudden; so utterly without reason. If their friends wondered why Nancy had carelessly let him dart out on the ramp, they didn't say so. And probably no one even realized Paul could have simply flicked off the magnetos when he first saw the boy running, and maybe, just maybe, the propeller would have stopped in time.

Those days after the funeral when Paul and

Nancy tried to settle down to the routine of life, it dawned on him with pitiless finality that the boy was really gone. He was in heaven with Christ, yes; but how Paul missed him here! On Sunday afternoons he had sometimes borrowed Savillas's mare, and he and Eddy had trotted up and down the sandy streets of this German Mennonite colony, past the adobe houses with their tile roofs, with Eddy laughing that chuckly little laugh of his. Now how empty were these hours! Added to his grief, a cancerous fear began to grow within him. His carelessness had killed. Could it ever happen again? Tomorrow? Next year?

One morning, riding to the airfield in Savillas's jeep, Paul unburdened this growing phobia to his friend. Until that time he had told no one, for Paul Graham was a man having many friends but few close ones, and Savillas was one of the few. A brother in Christ, he shared the bond of flight as well, operating a flying safari service out of Colonia. As they drove up the sandy street, laid out, with typical German precision, as straight as an arrow, past the still functional hitching posts, Savillas's dark eyes fixed his friend with a baleful stare. "Paulo, if you had switched off the magnetos, the propeller would have continued for two or more revolutions, would it not? Thus the tragedy was unavoidable. It would have occurred no matter. Why do you afflict yourself for no reason?" It was a response typical of Savillas, whose buoyancy was more characteristic of a Brazilian Carioca than a normally reserved Paraguayan.

"But the point is," Paul protested, "I didn't even think of it. I just sat there like an idiot. I froze. And what if I should ever freeze like that in the air?"

"You were tired then. And it came unexpectedly."

"It's certain I'll be tired again sometime."

"Paulo," Savillas shook his head in exasperation. "We have all experienced— The problem is, we pretend we are God, infallible. Should it disturb you to find you are only a man after all?"

Paul envied Savillas. Not that his friend was careless in the least, but it seems some pilots wear their responsibility more easily than others. Your passengers? Get your own self down in one piece, and they will automatically follow. But for Paul it was not that easy. He knew that for those who trusted him in the air, it was his judgement, his movements of the controls that insured a safe return to the world they had left. This responsibility was the magnificent isolation that had once been the joy but now was the curse of his flying.

Dr. Pearson read from the Bible—The book of Romans—and his voice was as compassionate and gentle as the circle of yellow light bathing them from the kerosene lamp. "'And we know that all things work together for good to them that love God, to them who are the called according to his purpose.'* 'O the depth of the riches both of the wisdom and knowledge of God! how unsearchable are his judgements, and his ways past finding out! For who hath known the mind of the Lord, or who hath been his counselor?'"†

Pearson looked up and tried to ignore the increasing hostility in Nancy's girlish face. "Nancy, you're a servant of the Lord. You've known these Scriptures for years. They're basic, aren't they?"

She nodded silently. Yes, she knew them and felt she was being mocked by them now.

"So it obviously isn't enough to just know this, is it? That God is all wise, that He works all things together for our good. No, we must go a step further." The pages crackled in the silence as he turned to another passage and read. "'And not only so, but we glory in tribulation also: knowing that tribulation worketh patience; and patience, experience; and experience, hope.'"‡ His smile to them was radiant. "Think of that, Paul and Nancy. We Christians can actually rejoice in our troubles! And why? Because God can use them to make us better servants! And that is not a privilege to be taken lightly, especially in view of eternity. Now, Nancy, certainly when

---
*Romans 8:28.
†Romans 11:33-34.
‡Romans 5:3-4.

you became a missionary you surrendered your life completely to the Lord. What I'm going to ask you will be hard, but it's necessary. Are you willing to thank the Lord for the benefits He will give you from your sorrow?"

A wave rippled through her reddish-brown hair as her head snapped erect. "Dr. Pearson, you didn't see the blood! You didn't see Eddy with his head split—" She burst into tears again, and Paul's stomach wrenched. "I see that every time I close my eyes!" she sobbed. "I would be insane to thank God for doing that!"

"Nancy, we don't know that God caused this to happen—"

"We know He allowed it!"

"Yes, and for a reason that is your ultimate good, and Paul's. We must look beyond this tragedy to the ultimate good."

"No. I can't believe that now." She gazed imploringly at Dr. Pearson. Nancy's large brown eyes glistened in the lamplight. "Dr. Pearson, why does God think it's necessary to torment the people who are trying to serve Him? Look at the ones who never raise a finger to do His work. Nothing bad ever happens to them! No, I can't thank Him. I can't even pray to Him anymore."

"There's a reason you can't pray, Nancy. Do you realize, according to the things you've just said, apparently you feel morally superior to God? If you feel this way, how can He possibly help you?"

She eyed the old gentleman and Paul defiantly. "I can't help the way I feel."

A shiver ran through Paul then, and Travis Pearson removed his glasses to rub his eyes. The Grahams' spiritual condition was much more serious than he had supposed. Serious enough to be fatal to their Christian service if not soon conquered. And what a tragedy for the young couple. What a tragedy for Interior Evangelism to lose its valuable pilot.

Paul had played a key role with the mission, more important than he sometimes realized. It had been founded twelve years ago by Dr. Pearson and several other experienced missionaries to whom the Lord had given a heart burden for the fifty thousand Moro, Lengua, and Edigo Indians scattered throughout the Chaco. "The tragedy of it," Dr. Pearson often said, "is that these Indians at one time knew God, for their tradition indicates that they worshiped God as a Spirit. If there were only someone to go to them, they could know Him again." Dr. Pearson detested half measures. He had organized a series of permanent outpost missions staffed by hardy souls who shared his same burden for the Indians' salvation. And Paul Graham with his airplane was the lifeline of these outposts, reaching in hours stations that would take weeks to reach by land.

But the Lord's work is never done except it draws fire from the enemy, and Paul and Nancy walked dejectedly into the whispering darkness while the heartbroken Pearsons watched them go. Through the warm night drifted the sweet, haunting music of a Paraguayan harp, accompanied by throaty Guarani lyrics. Puente, the Mission's maintenance man, who kept his room upstairs in the brick headquarters house, was singing, and Paul hoped that he had heard none of their stormy counseling session.

But the Indian had heard, and he ceased playing momentarily as the Grahams' footsteps echoed across the wooden veranda below. Yes, he had heard. And his heart was troubled and perplexed. How was it possible Paul Graham or his wife should not find all the comfort they needed in the Lord Jesus? Was the Lord Jesus failing? No, such a thing was impossible; for Puente was a converted alcoholic; and who but the mighty Lord Christ could have conquered the evil of whiskey in his life and given him such happiness that even his ravaged face could reflect it? *"Thou wilt keep him in perfect peace, whose mind is stayed on thee: because he trusteth in thee."*[§] The verse from Isaiah came to Puente's thoughts. No, it was not God who was failing; and Puente was forced to the painful conclusion: the fault must lie with Paul Graham, his Christian brother and friend. Puente sighed and surveyed his collection of ornate *bombilla*

[§]Isaiah 26:3

gourds. Many times he and Paulo had drunk *yerba mate,* the strong Paraguayan tea, from the same *bombilla;* this was the sign of true friendship in Paraguay. How sad it was now to see his friend no longer rejoicing in the Lord!

Puente liked to adapt himself to the people around him. With his Christian brother Savillas, he was loud, even a fool. But with Paul Graham, Puente would be quietly helpful. Each morning they would roll the blue and white DeVoss B from its hangar, and it would sit nose high like a horse sniffing the wind. And as they loaded the airplane, Puente did not mind when Paul, scowling behind his sunglasses, rechecked the straps holding cans of kerosene and diesel oil. For who would want flammable oil splashing around in his airplane? Puente understood and was not insulted.

Just this morning, he remembered, as they loaded the plane, Nancy Graham had glided past on her bicycle, on her way to the office radio room, where she would follow her husband's flights over the wilderness. Even though Paul had watched her move out of sight around the house, she had neither waved nor looked toward the hated airplane. Puente had noticed Paul's scowl and grunted softly to himself. Of what use is beauty if the woman's spirit is cold?

Now he heard them leave the house and decided tonight he must pray much for them.

It could have been a good night, a magic night,

as Paul and Nancy paused outside their rented adobe house on Calle Palma and dipped a cool drink from the concrete cistern running along its eaves; for the night was warm and perfumed and alive, and she was gently outlined in the light from a half moon. But it was not to be. She lay to herself on her side of the bed, cold and inaccessible, loath to stay awake but afraid to sleep, for she would dream again of Eddy, and his little voice would echo through the ghostly corridors of her dreams.

"Paul, I want to quit," she said suddenly, and it startled him, for he had thought she was asleep. "I want to quit and go home, and we'll have Eddy's body taken away from here, and we'll bury him on the hill at home." Paul knew that she was speaking of the small cemetery on her family's farm in Virginia's Catawba Valley, a place that her heart had never really left.

"Nancy, let's not talk about that now, please! We can't decide anything now, not in the shape we're in."

"I've already decided," she said simply. "There's nothing for me here, is there? Except—"

"Me?"

She didn't answer, and Paul sighed in exasperation. "This has been a rough evening. We'll talk in the morning, OK?"

"Why wait till morning? What will change in the morning?"

"I suppose nothing, unless God comes down and personally apologizes to you. I tell you, I'm surprised Pearson didn't refer us to the book of Job for a good example."

He thought of Job's words, *"Though he slay me, yet will I trust him."*[1] Paul harbored no illusions. Plainly their faith wasn't in the same league as Job's. "But think about it, Nancy," he said, making a stab at rationality. "Do you think you and I would ever be content just to settle on the farm? I can't see that at all."

"I can see it, and I like it. Why not?"

That was a good question. To be sure, she had been happy enough there before they were married. He remembered the summer he and Nancy had met; the summer they both served as counselors at a Christian camp for inner-city slum children. At summer's end he had visited Nancy and her parents at the Sheffield farm for several days. She was supremely happy just being there. Clad in blue jeans and a red blouse, she had guided him around; she had even showed him how to milk a cow one evening. Her silvery laughter rang with girlish delight as she squirted milk into the cat's mouth while the cat blinked and licked its whiskers.

Later they sat together on a hilltop to watch as, across the valley, night crept into the folds and hollows of Catawba Mountain. The waning sun

---

[1] Job 13:15.

cast an orange glow on her tanned face, partially hidden in wisps of reddish brown hair. He thought he had never in all his life seen anyone as beautiful as this elfish girl who could find such delight at squirting milk in a cat's mouth.

"You know," she had said at length, "those kids, those poor kids we worked with this summer. How many of them ever get to see a sight like this and know peace like this?"

"I know what you mean," he said.

"It was frightening in a way, wasn't it? I mean, they were so pathetic; they were so eager to know love. It was like a foreign thing to them. Some of my kids didn't even know who their parents were."

"But a lot of them came to know Christ's love this summer, didn't they?" Paul smiled.

"Yes, they did. But now camp is over, and they have to go back to that same old life, and what chance will their faith have to grow? They'll be surrounded by so many others who don't know Christ, and who will probably never know Him. And if this continues, Paul, whatever will become of our country? Every day all summer I would break up fights and try to manage explosive kids who had no idea what authority or love is. And some nights I'd have nightmares. I'd dream about riots in the city and burning buildings—stuff like that. I know it sounds funny, but I did."

He was silent, pleased simply to have her share her thoughts with him.

"And Paul, that's why I wonder sometimes if it's really logical to plan for mission work in another country when Christians are needed so much here."

"I've thought about that myself this summer—thought about it a lot. But Nancy, here's my conclusion. Our country is really saturated with the Gospel, after all. There are Bibles everywhere. And all a person has to do is flick on the radio or TV on a Sunday morning and, you know, he'll hear some junk, but the truth will be there, too. But these Indians I've been telling you about—some of them have nobody, nobody at all who can even tell them the plan of salvation in their own language. And as far as I'm concerned, the Lord is the Commander in this. He has given me the desire to fly for Him, and the ability to do it. And it's in the isolated areas missionary pilots are most needed, not in this country."

"Maybe—maybe it's just that the experiences at camp are still so fresh in my mind."

"That's what I like about you," he grinned. "You never learned that it's stupid to get involved."

"Look who's talking!" She flicked some grass in his face, but he only brushed it aside, suddenly serious.

"Nancy," he said. "I have no doubt about what the Lord wants of my life, but if we plan to get married, there should be no doubt in your mind, either. Have you claimed our verse on this?"

She had smiled and quoted their verse word for word, her clear voice caressing the quiet hilltop. "'Trust in the LORD with all thine heart; and lean not unto thine own understanding. In all thy ways acknowledge him, and he will direct thy paths.'"# She wrinkled her nose at him. "Don't worry; I'll be sure before I marry you. But there is something I'm sure of right now." She reached out to kiss him. "I love you."

If Nancy had experienced doubts about foreign service at first, they were trivial compared to those of her parents. After dinner that evening they lingered, talking around the table in the huge farm kitchen while Annie Sheffield blanched beans for the freezer. Paul watched the spry little woman work amid clouds of steam billowing to the ceiling, her red, rough hands speaking eloquently of the work involved in this place, and he sensed that behind her energetic labor there was a nervousness.

"It's not that we're against you and Nancy getting married," she said. "You know that. Harless and I have prayed that when Nancy gets married, it will be to a fine Christian man like you. Heaven knows we've seen enough—like them Smith girls. Married shiftless bums, every one of 'em lazy as hounds, and drinkin' and bed

---
#Proverbs 3:5-6.

hoppin' all over the county. But when you start this talk about taking our Nancy off to who-knows-where to help a tribe of Indians! Where'd you get such a notion, Paul?"

Paul laughed easily, pleased that his voice remained so relaxed. "From the Bible, Mrs. Sheffield. The same Bible you read every night." And he quoted the Lord's orders in Mark 16:15, "'Go ye into all the world, and preach the gospel to every creature.'"

"Oh, I know, I know all that. But Paul, what makes you think God wants you to go so far as that? God hasn't come down and said anything to you."

No, He had not nor was it necessary for Him to do so. Paul tried hard to explain a concept beyond words: the first tuggings within his spirit; growing desire to serve the Lord at whatever cost; the joy of seeing his own ambition to fly fall into line with the Lord's will, as evidenced by a quiet conscience and a jubilant spirit; and at last the thrill of seeing his faith confirmed as the Lord opened doors of opportunity and arranged events as no human ever could. This, then, was the growth process by which he knew he would fly for the Lord somewhere—probably serving Indian tribes in South America.

"Humph!" she said. "You talk just like Nancy, and you're both too sensible for that. Those Indians have their own ways. Leave them alone.

They've got along just fine for a thousand years, haven't they?"

"That's just the point." Paul's voice became dead serious now. "They haven't gotten along; they aren't getting along at all. They live in fear you wouldn't believe, Mrs. Sheffield. They see an evil spirit in the wine jar or in the blanket, and they have to appease these spirits with unbelievably cruel rituals. Most of them have no law except a code of revenge and fear—no mercy or love. Then, all their lives, it's just one disease after another. Finally they die and go out into the darkness—without a chance to hear of God's salvation. I don't call that 'getting along' at all. I mean, we have the light of God's Word, and it's just inconceivable to me that we would keep it from those who don't have it."

They were silent a moment, somewhat subdued by the unexpected force of Paul's answer. Annie Sheffield sniffed and irritably shook down a plastic bag of beans, giving several hard shakes as if she were beating back the logic he had thrown at her.

"Now, you've had trainin' and I haven't, and I ain't fixed to argue with you. But at least common sense is on my side." She turned to them, smiling unexpectedly. "And besides, if you go off to South America, you won't get any more of this apple cake."

They had all laughed then. But Paul had

sensed, in spite of the laughter, the resistance of Nancy's parents, unyielding as stone.

Nancy's voice suddenly jerked him from these memories back to the problem at hand. "I'm not too proud to go back home." Her words echoed flat in the darkness.

"Pride has nothing to do with it!" he snapped. "This is our *life*, Nancy. If we give this up, what have we got? You and I have to lick this thing. We have to wait on the Lord."

"And wait, and wait, and wait—"

Her taunt broke Paul, and he rose abruptly from the bed and stalked into the kitchen. This could not be happening to him! Hoping to drown the butterflies in his stomach, he poured a glass of tepid milk from the icebox. They had planned to buy a bottled-gas refrigerator one day, but it appeared they would not be needing it, now.

And in the night, he tried to loose himself with the promises of Psalm 91:1-3, 15:

> He that dwelleth in the secret place of the most High shall abide under the shadow of the Almighty. I will say of the LORD, He is my refuge and my fortress: my God; in him will I trust. Surely he shall deliver thee from the snare of the fowler, And from the noisome pestilence.
>
> I will be with him in trouble; I will deliver him, and honour him.

The words left him strangely cold. Outside, the

Assassin's Wind, the hot, dry wind from north toward the equator, whistled down darkened Calle Palma. *Tomorrow again, Senor Graham, it hissed. We will ride the sky together. I will bounce your airplane, maybe send you into a tree on take-off, eh?*

To quit. Simply to quit. It would be so easy, and the idea flooded him with a strange comfort. But no, he would fly tomorrow, and the next day, and the next. Instinctively he knew that if he surrendered to the ogre of doubt, he would never again find the courage to break its grip.

3

Satan Is Not Easily Defeated at Asoe

Paul lowered half flaps and cruised lazily over the six-hundred-foot airstrip, a grassy clearing hacked from the jungle near Asoe. This preliminary inspection was standard procedure since the time he had flown straight into the clearing and been startled by four small deer bounding down the runway like graceful ghosts, barely ahead of his plane. Now, low fuel or not, he buzzed the runway. The crude windsock hung limp. Well, that was a mixed blessing—good because with no wind, the runway would be an easier target; bad because there would be no headwind to slow his groundspeed on landing.

He opened the throttle and circled up and around the village, looking down his wing at the clustered grass-roofs below, and flew out about two miles before turning to make his approach. In turbulent air, Paul liked a long, unhurried approach—get the cockpit fiddling done, and be free to concentrate on flying the bird in. His errant thoughts momentarily forgotten, as he knew they would be, he flicked his hands across the instrument panel in tense concentration, readying the plane for landing. *Fuel selector valve switched to the wing tank containing the most fuel; fuel boost pump, on; carburetor heat, on; mixture, full rich; throttle lock, free.* He advanced the propeller control to flat pitch, and the engine whined upward like a quickened pulse, telling the pilot that playtime was over.

A mile from touchdown and four hundred feet in the air, with the green carpet of Quinee Pede drifting beneath him, he saw his target, the airstrip, bobbing in the windshield as his plane bucked and wallowed in the air currents. "OK, Graham, old boy, let's get a glass of water from Elmer Fudd," he muttered. Pulling the throttle back and holding the nose level, he began to slow his speed; the slipstream died to a whisper. *Ninety miles an hour. Eighty.* He lowered full flaps and continued to slow to his approach speed of sixty-five miles an hour.

Airspeed: the harsh master of every pilot. There is, in the design of every aircraft wing, a speed known as the "stall speed." Below this speed the wing can no longer produce lift, and the plane falls like a stone. It is on this tightrope the bush pilot earns his bread; he must sense, almost instinctively like a bird, the workings of thrust, drag, lift, and gravity. And he must slow his plane to its slowest possible speed and yet stay above the deadly stall. For Paul Graham's DeVoss, this stall speed with full flaps down was fifty-five miles an hour.

The runway was drawing closer now. Paul kept the end of it fixed in his windshield, jockeying the rudder and ailerons in perfect coordination, compensating for each updraft with a matching adjustment of the throttle so his engine rose and fell in a moaning refrain. Imperceptibly raising and lowering the aircraft's nose, he kept the airspeed glued on sixty-five miles an hour, not by observing the gauge but by feel, with that honed instinct of the veteran bush pilot. The old-timer's adage flashed perversely into his thoughts, *take your stall speed, add ten miles per hour for your wife, five for each kid.*

"Yeah," he muttered. "I've got ten for you, Nancy. And five for—" OK, five for the next baby they would have when Nancy got over her rotten self-pity.

Watch it, kid! The runway that had been coming lazily closer was now rushing into the windshield. *Right on target, but a little high and fast.* He hauled up the nose and flared out like a huge hawk, his landing gear feeling for the ground. *Too fast!* He was eating up the runway like a cannonball express, with brush and trees rushing toward him at frightening speed. *Too late to go around. Hold the nose back—* The wheels finally touched down. Instantly Paul raised the flaps, thus settling the plane's weight fully on its wheels, and then stood on the brakes, preparing to pivot around in a groundloop if necessary. *Better to prang a wing tip than plow through the trees—* But it wasn't necessary, and the DeVoss slithered to a halt with barely thirty feet to spare.

For heaven's sake, Graham! Watch what you're doing! he scolded himself. He had had no business thinking of Nancy and Eddy just then, no business at all. He cut the engine and sat for a moment in the suddenly stifling cockpit, listening to the dying whine of the gyrocompass and hoping his nerves would wind down with it.

But he was not to be allowed that respite. The missionary, Fucelli, erupted from the afternoon forest shadows, his face taut. With him stumbled and ran his five-year-old daughter, Laurie, reflecting with a solemn face her father's anxiety, and behind them surged the usual brown mob of naked children coming to see the *Chuchabasui* (the thing that falls).

Fucelli jerked the cockpit door open. "Come on, Paul," he rasped, "don't just sit there. Why, I'd be shaky, too, if I nearly mowed down half the jungle!" Normally Fucelli greeted Paul with a cold glass of water from the kerosene refrigerator. But today there was no drink and no jokes from the bald-headed missionary, nicknamed Elmer Fudd after that cartoon character with the same feature. Today, with sweat soaking his khaki shirt and trousers, he was all business. "Get the stretcher, man, and come on. We've got troubles, Paul."

"That bad?" Paul asked quietly, as he eased from the cockpit.

"Oh, man! If Campemai dies, this place will be a no man's land. And it'll take a surgeon to get that lance point out of him."

Voluble and uninhibited as ever, the children clustered around Paul as he unloaded the stretcher, thrusting their hands into his pockets to see what treasures were there, and seemingly unconcerned that their fathers might soon be at war with the Edigo-Koro. *No peppermints!* Paul shrugged his shoulders and knuckled the straight, black hair on a few heads, unable to tell them that he had not planned on flying out here so soon and thus had no candy.

In the Edigo-Sota village of adobe, grass-roofed huts, smoke pungent with the smell of roast armadillo drifted through slanting shafts of afternoon sunlight. Usually, Paul's landings at Asoe were accompanied by chattering and shoulder slapping, the Edigo's handshake equivalent, but now the village was quiet. In front of their huts, several women sitting before the cooking fires eyed Paul and the stretcher, and they wailed softly in apprehension. There was not a man to be seen. From several hundred yards out in the jungle echoed the staccatto *rat-*

a-tat of a woodpecker on a hollow ironwood tree. But it was not a woodpecker, and Paul felt the hair rise on the back of his neck.

"The signal corps," said Fucelli wryly. "Inacarai has his men spread out in a battle line. I think the drummer was telling him where their flanks are, how close they are to the Koro. I was just over at the Koro village, and they're spread out in the woods too. They'll probably stay that way all night, because neither side wants to cluster in the village, where they'd be sitting ducks. They have odd ideas about fighting."

"Yeah," Paul said thickly. He shook his head. Only moments before, he had been seated before a twentieth-century instrument panel, and now he was walking into a timeless land of bow, spear, and drum signals. A vague feeling of time disjointed, which always crept over him at Asoe, was more intense than ever in the wailing quiet.

"I don't think the Koro want to fight," Fucelli went on. "Inacarai is a famous tactician, and he's slaughtered them too many times over the years. So if there's war, this side will probably start it. And," Fucelli breathed deeply, "if Inacarai's son dies, he won't hesitate a minute."

The children had left them, and Laurie ran ahead to the longhouse. Outside, several of Inacarai's lieutenants stood guard, armed with bows, arrows, and lances. Paul noted that they were cruel, man-killing lances, tipped with hardwood, barbed points, which could not be withdrawn from a victim but must be pushed the rest of the way through and the shaft cut. He shuddered to think that it was this type of point now imbedded in the chest of Campemai.

Unlike some tribes, The Edigo shun war ceremonies. Thus the guards who admitted them to the longhouse wore only the standard leather string and flaps; only Inacarai wore a ceremonial war bonnet of feathers from the white hawk and parrot. Seated on a mat of jaguar pelts, his face hard as flint and his eyes smoldering with betrayed trust, the old chief seemed scarcely to notice Paul and Fucelli but kept his eyes fixed on the mat where Campemai lay, bathed in sweat, his breath coming in painful heaves. Fucelli's handsome, brunette wife had propped the chief's son on his side with pillows, so that blood would accumulate in the lung already punctured. She had bandaged the wound tightly to prevent its sucking air, but this had also stopped the drainage of blood. Thus Campemai was faced with the cruel choice of suffocating now or, in a few hours, drowning in his own blood.

"Pray, Paul," the missionary whispered. "Inacarai isn't taking this well at all."

Paul uttered one of the few Edigo phrases he knew, a gutteral greeting to the chief, and then stepped aside as Fucelli asked permission to take Campemai on the *Chuchabasui*.

Both men grew uneasy at this unusual quiet of

the normally garrulous Edigo, for Inacarai's expression did not change. His intelligent, leathered face betrayed none of his soul's struggle. Finally he nodded up and down, meaning no. Campemai must stay in the longhouse.

Fucelli's heart plummeted, and he guessed the reason immediately. "Will Paje-de work magic tonight?" he asked sharply.

Inacarai, a professing Christian, would not meet Fucelli's eyes. Yes, Paje-de, the sorcerer, would come tonight and witch the sickness and lance from Campemai in an eleborate, drunken ceremony. Inacarai, whether in desperation, senility, or anger, when the crisis had come was falling back on the old powers, and his son would not be allowed aboard the "falling thing."

Let those who have never wrestled with fear and superstition say they are easily conquered. There was a place in the jungle where Paje-de had driven into the ground a red Quebracho stake: a monument to the place and time his life had been possessed by an evil spirit. Fucelli knew the place, and he knew Paje-de's influence and power were frighteningly real. Marilyn looked up at her husband, her eyes, as dark as the Indian's, plainly asking "now what?"

Fucelli did not know, and for a moment he stared at the stubborn chief. *Lord, I trust you*, he prayed silently, simply. *I don't know what to do, Father. Show me.* It was well Fucelli should pray, for all that he had worked for in the last four years was in danger of being destroyed at that moment. *It can't end this way!* How was it possible he could have so misjudged Inacarai's faith?

Fucelli knew Inacarai and the Edigo well, for he was the first outsider to have lived any length of time with these elusive hunters who range through the Chaco areas of Paraguay, Bolivia, and Argentina. Perhaps he had succeeded when others failed because he had come with an interpreter, a stocky Edigo named Yocai, who had been captured several years before in a military raid. Yocai translated both Spanish and Guarani into the Edigo language, and he was valuable as a cultural buffer between the missionary couple and their sometimes inexplicable Edigo.

Leaving Laurie at Colonia, Ed and Marilyn had moved in with the Indians in the spring of 1970. On Yocai's advice they chose Asoe, for here were the headquarters of Inacarai, chief of the Edigo-Sota, the dominant faction of a tribe racked by sporadic warfare since, as the ancients said, all things had begun. Why the almost casual killing of their fellow Edigo? "They are the 'pig people,'" Inacarai said simply. "Unfit to live." And Fucelli dreamed of the day he could unite the Edigo in Christ's love.

The first months had been good ones for Fucelli, in some ways. There had been the heady thrill of being accepted by the Indians, who, with their stocky bodies and wide, pinched eyes, resembled sub-tropical Eskimoes. Sociable and impulsive, Fucelli was quite compatible with his boisterous hosts; and with a better knowledge of the language, the gravel-voiced missionary could soon banter hilariously with them, or at least try. He made endless discoveries, such as how the Edigo sometimes change their names at the birth of their children. An Indian whom Fucelli knew as "Peijai" could one day suddenly become "Pejnoco-de," or "father of Pejnoco." It was confusing, but then, Fucelli reasoned, free of the governmental computers that plague more organized societies, the Edigo could change their names any time they felt like it. After the couple had brought their daughter out to live with them, the Indians named Ed "Laujai-de," or "Father of Laurie." "It sounds better than Bwana," Marilyn laughed.

On a night during the brief, rainy winter, they had made another discovery, this one about Edigo marriage customs. They had been asked to shelter a dispossessed wife. Yocai explained it all quite casually to a baffled Ed Fucelli the next day. Among the Edigo, it is the woman who chooses her own mate. Sometimes an Edigo woman will change husbands two or three times during her life. A young single woman will usually follow the men out on hunt and offer herself to a prospective husband of her choice. If he is pleased with her, she becomes his wife. Trouble comes, Yocai said, when a woman offers herself to a married man. If he prefers her over his old wife, the old wife is evicted from the hut, sometimes brutally. It was one of these dispossessed wives the missionary couple cared for that night. It was easy to sympathize with her wails until they learned that three years earlier she had stolen the man from someone else.

Those had been months of learning and discovery, full of joy and riddled with homesickness and discouragement. Paul Graham would airdrop food and medicine. They would listen to Laurie's baby-talk over the battery-powered shortwave and ache to see her. They dispensed shots, bandages, and sympathy for spider and snake bites, scorpion stings, and lance wounds. They suffered from mosquitoes and painful sores left by ravenous ticks.

Most of Ed's time had been taken in clearing an airstrip from the endless scrub jungle. He and the Indians had hacked through thickly grown *cardinioso* and *quinee pede*, trees loaded with hooked thorns that grabbed anything brushing against them. Fucelli soon learned why the Edigo distain clothing in general, for everything he wore was soon ripped to shreds.

Before the airstrip was ready, Ed had come down with dysentery. He had recovered. But just as the runway was completed he had become sick again, this time with malaria during the torrid summer. How ironic that the first patient to be flown out of Asoe had been Fucelli himself! And Dr. Pearson, as he visited his thin, sweating, and shivering colleague in the clinic, had remarked, "Now you're beginning to look like a missionary."

Ah, but with the completion of the airstrip, the big hurdle had been crossed. Talking into a box through the air, *the Coijone* could call down the "falling thing" loaded with medicine and the wonderful-tasting new food. And the Indians were awed. With Paul Graham ferrying material in, Ed and Marilyn had constructed a small house complete with adobe walls, screening, and a tin roof. To ward off the hated ticks, they had plastered the outside of it with an insect-repelling mixture of sand, clay, and cow manure, copying a technique used on the older German houses in Colonia. When the mixture dried it could be painted, and there was no odor. Next came luxuries as a ten-kilowatt-hour diesel generator, a kerosene refrigerator, and even a small tractor to keep the airstrip mowed.

By any standards they had come a long way; yet one day, as they were praying and studying together, Ed and Marilyn had been forced to a painful conclusion. Their mission, for all its outward signs of success, was really accomplishing very little. The Edigo, for some reason, had remained completely indifferent to the Gospel of Jesus Christ. They would listen to the story of Jesus because it was interesting, but they resisted the truth that He had died for their souls.

Yocai told Fucelli why. "It is Paje-de," he

said. "He is telling us to refuse your words about *Jesus Uje Chignorai*, for we will die if we worship your God." So the intertribal warfare continued, as did the wife trading and evicting, and the killing of unhealthy babies. Worst of all, the Edigo remained slaves of fearful spirits represented by Paje-de and those like him, while they shunned faith in Christ, which could free them.

Many were his sleepless nights as Fucelli had lain thinking and wondering, watching the fat lizards clinging to his screen, silhouetted against the stars, as they gorged on mosquitoes. And he would pray for a miracle. The Lord had begun answering his prayers in an unexpected way when, one day in the summer, Yocai invited *Laujai-de* to go pig hunting with him and seven other warriors. Marilyn had watched them go with trepidation, for many hunting parties returned carrying not only game but also injured comrades, victims of boar tusks or snake bite on the trail. Ed soon learned he could never keep up with the warriors, who could trail their loping dogs for hours without tiring, and he and Yocai fell ever farther behind. Yocai could not hide his irritation at his slow friend. "We will not bring you to hunt the jaguar," he said. "For the *coijone* doesn't know the jaguar." Fucelli readily agreed that he did not.

That afternoon they overtook their companions at a wadi where the dogs had cornered something. Even before reaching the scene of action, Yocai could tell by the hounds' frantic baying that it was not a herd of the small white pigs, but a large, black boar: the *chauche negre.* "It is the large, dangerous one," he informed a sweating and scratched Fucelli. And so Fucelli had witnessed a stone-age drama seen by few outsiders, as the sharpshooters, Jamai and Yocamai-de, shot arrow after arrow into the enraged, screaming boar. And when it was sufficiently weakened, all the men waded in to finish it off with hardwood clubs in a bloody finale.

Flushed with success, they had camped that night beside an open, grassy plain, and Fucelli had fallen into that same timeless limbo known by Paul Graham. Was it a thousand years ago, before the Spanish came? Who could tell? For out here there was no sign that Spain or Europe ever existed. Christ could even now be walking the streets of Nazareth; the Edigo had been here then. These timeless men, perhaps camping in this very spot while the same eternal, brilliant stars shone in their dark eyes. And Christ's death had been for them as for all men.

"We want you to tell us again of *Jesus Uje Chignorai,*" Yocai had said. In the firelight were eight Indian faces, eager, intent. And suddenly Fucelli knew why he had been invited on this hunt. Out here, away from the ever-present gaze of Paje-de, the men wanted to listen. Their spirits were stirred by the amazing words of Jesus; they hungered to hear more.

The missionary's heart had soared. Yocai threw pieces of termite nest on the fire to repel mosquitoes, and Fucelli began to tell the Gospel, the Good News. The Edigo understood the principle of offering sacrifice. It seems that the truth of Romans 3:23, "For all have sinned, and come short of the glory of God," is instinctively known by all men, primitive or modern. All men vaguely sense that a higher power is not pleased with their sins and imperfections. The primitive man offers sacrifices of animals and riches, even mutilates his own body to mollify the spirits. An Edigo will pluck out his eyebrows and lashes. The modern man endures a sermon or some other religious ritual and gives to the community fund. Yet both know that this is not enough, not nearly enough.

Fucelli had told of the only God, who had made the stars and the Edigo themselves. How could any sacrifice win the favor of such a one? He had told of heaven, where there was only peace and happiness and no war or killing. "How can you go to this wonderful place when you hate the 'pig people' and want to kill them? There is too much wickedness in your hearts to ever go there."

And the hunters had been deeply troubled.

Then he had told the Good News of *Jesus Uje Chignorai*, God's own Son, who had come from heaven. Fucelli had read the first verse he had ever translated into Edigo, John 3:16: "For God so loved the world, that he gave His only begotten Son, that whosoever believeth in him should not perish, but have everlasting life." He had told how Jesus Himself had died as a sacrifice, the only sacrifice that would please the great God of heaven. "Jesus' sacrifice paid for your evil. Now you can ask Jesus to take away your wickedness. If you ask Him, His Spirit will come to live in your spirit. Because He is the only sacrifice that pleases God, God will be pleased with you as well. God will become your Father. He will clean the wickedness from your heart and stomach. He will give you love for the 'pig people.' And when you die, your spirit will go to the heaven in peace."

The hunters had been incredulous. Such a thing had never been known. To love an enemy! And yet— "My heart is hurting," said Yocai.

That was how the miracle had begun. Yocai and three other warriors had surrendered their lives to Christ that night, and from this nucleus of four the faith in Jesus Christ had begun to grow. Paje-de had been powerless to stop its slow but inexorable spread through the tribe. When the famous old chief, Inacarai, had publicly taken Jesus as his sacrifice and *Wasai*, Fucelli had been guardedly jubilant. But the change in Inacarai's life had proved to be real, for shortly afterward he had ordered his warriors to cease harassing the Edigo-Koro. As a further step of peace, he had even invited his former enemies to settle near Asoe, so they, too, could be near the *Coijone* missionaries. This concern for the welfare of a once hated foe was proof to Fucelli that Inacarai had experienced a genuine conversion.

The latest triumph of faith involved Fucelli's interpreter, and now good friend, Yocai. Ijomejene, the wife of Yocai, had a baby who had been sickly and weak from birth, a useless child. Only a year ago he would have been dropped into a shallow grave and forgotten. But as Christ grows and flourishes in a human soul, like a rose from sterile ground, there grows also a concern for even useless, troublesome life. They had begged Fucelli to save the baby, and Paul Graham had flown him and Ijomejene to the Colonia clinic, where they were now being cared for. This was the stuff of dreams, and Fucelli was awed at how completely the Lord had answered his prayer.

But Satan was not to be easily defeated at Asoe. Campemai and a Koro hunter had contested who was entitled to a jaguar pelt, an Edigo symbol of masculinity. The fight, swift and savage, had left Campemai dying of a barbed lance in his chest. And the eyes of Inacarai smoldered. His trust was betrayed by those with whom he had made peace. "Once I forgave them for Jesus," he spat. "I will not do it again."

"Will men say Inacarai made peace with the

Koro," Fucelli asked, "so he could easily kill them?"

Inacarai flared. Had he made peace with them so they could kill his son?

"Campemai isn't dead yet," Fucelli rasped. "But he will surely die if we cannot take him to the sickhouse where Ijomejene and her baby are now being made well."

Would the *Coijone* turn his hand (make a promise) to save Campemai?

Fucelli paused, for Inacarai's faith, like a new plant, was tender and easily crushed. If he refused to promise results, the chief would surely keep his son and rely on Paje-de's magic. But if he promised Campemai would live and the youth died, would Inacarai ever trust the missionaries again?

"Do you remember," Fucelli asked softly, "that Jesus will do what is best with your life? I cannot promise that your son will live. I trust Jesus to do the best thing. You must trust Him too."

Inacarai again shook his head up and down. No, he must have a promise.

Sweat rolled from Fucelli in the stifling heat. "Is Inacarai a chief of falsehood? Will you break your treaty with the Koro and your treaty with Jesus as well? You know the power of Paje-de is evil. In your anger you are acting like a child."

The chief glared at Fucelli, for the missionary's words cut deeply. He nodded toward Marilyn and her medical bag, and his voice was cold with finality. Campemai must stay in the longhouse. He would accept medicine from the Coijone there, and accept magic from Paje-de also. He would trust both Jesus and the old powers; these were Inacarai's final words on the matter.

Fucelli was sickened. *Oh Father,* he prayed, *give me wisdom.* And an idea flashed into his mind even as he prayed. "We are leaving your longhouse!" he barked. "If you accept magic from Paje-de, we will not work medicine." He pointed to Campemai's tightly bandaged ribs. "Blood will fill his chest. He will die, and Paje-de cannot save him!"

Inacarai's eyes darted to Marilyn, then back to Fucelli. He was wavering.

"Trust Jesus and no one else," said Fucelli softly.

The chief rose to his feet, plainly furious at being thus trapped. He paced toward Marilyn, then back. Then, to make it appear he was still in charge of the situation, he stalked to the door and jerked back the skin, motioning savagely to Fucelli. "Take him on the *Chuchabasui!*" he growled. "Save his life, or I will kill all of your Koro *wasai!*"

Followed by a silent group of women and children, Paul and Fucelli carried Campemai's stretcher to the plane. Paul's nerves were taut, because the sun was getting low and he still had to detour to Bahia Negra for fuel, if indeed there was any fuel there. And if Alfredo had learned there was none— Well, Paul would figure the winds aloft carefully before takeoff, for there would be no margin for wandering around in the sky on this trip.

Fucelli's nerves twinged also in a sudden attack of doubt. Was he presuming on the Lord? Would it have been better to let Paje-de work his charms and when Campemai died, let the blame fall on the sorcerer and not the missionaries? Almost desperate, oblivious to any suggestion of caution, he was infected with restless impatience.

4

For Want of a Nail

For want of a nail a shoe was lost.
For want of a shoe a horse was lost.
For want of a horse a rider was lost.

In order to lay Campemai on his side, Marilyn had cut the lance shaft earlier in the day, and only two inches now protruded through the red-stained gauze. In solemn haste the missionaries propped their moaning patient with pillows, strapped him securely to the stretcher, then fastened the stretcher to special tie-downs on the floor. Fucelli would ride in the canvas jump seat beside Campemai, where he could monitor for airsickness, which, undetected, could strangle the Indian. Disturbed by Campemai's pain, Fucelli wished that the implacable foes of time and distance could somehow be overcome immediately. But alas, they could not.

While they worked, Paul slid into the pilot's seat and wiped the sweat from his forehead. *OK, he told himself, quiet down and think.* He could not let Campemai's delirious groans distract him; this must be a flight conducted like any other. He began calculating the velocity and direction of the winds aloft, values he must know before plotting the most direct heading to Colonia.

Marilyn jumped from the cargo door, and Fucelli slid it shut. "OK, let's go!"

"In a minute!" Paul said curtly.

Surprised, Fucelli looked over his pilot's shoulder, saw the winds aloft figures, and said no more. He wrote it off to nerves. They were both too tense.

Using the air speed and time en route from the flight he had just made, Paul calculated the vital figures. How good that the wind, so free and elemental, could be so easily captured by an X mark on the transparent azimuth of the Jeppesen flight computer. According to the little plastic instrument, the wind, at three thousand feet, was from two hundred degrees at thirty knots. He must point the nose at 210 degrees to offset its drift and should arrive over Colonia in an hour and thirty minutes. The pilot grimaced. A flight of that duration would leave the tanks bone dry. It was too close, much too close. But a detour to Bahia Negra for fuel would add at least forty-five minutes to their flight time, and with darkness falling in a little over two hours, even that choice was open to question.

Decision, choice, compromise: these are the stuff of a pilot's life. Though his decisions may be unnoticed by his passengers, their destinies are as much at stake as his own. Paul Graham made his choice. "Ed, we're going to take a little time to fly over to Bahia for gas. I mean, if they have any. We'll check with Alfredo as soon as we're off."

The thought of even a slight delay was unbearable to Fucelli. "You mean—we're out of gas?" He implored.

"We don't have quite enough, and it'll do Campemai no good if we run out of fuel on the way. The wind is against us. I'm sorry."

The missionary breathed out hard. "Well, let's get going." If he wondered why Paul had allowed the fuel supply to fall so low, he did not ask, and Paul did not bother explaining about the leaking prop seals of yesterday.

Good-byes were lost in the engine's starting clatter. Marilyn, Laurie, and a few Edigo women were out there waving, but they were no longer capable of being heard or touched, as if the simple act of starting the engine had propelled Paul and Fucelli into another level of existence. Marilyn blew a kiss to her husband as the plane began to move, and Paul envied him.

At the airstrip's end, grass and tree leaves bowed in waves with the passing prop blast as Paul kicked the tail around and locked the brakes for a short engine check. He revved the engine to eighteen hundred revolutions per minute to check out the magnetos and carburetor heat, then to two thousand revolutions per minute to run through the hydraulic pitch control. The engine whined upward as he returned the propeller to flat pitch and the DeVoss bucked and trembled in its own prop blast. It was a living thing eager to fly. *Fuel pressure and oil pressure OK. Manifold pressure, good.* The Lycoming was a good engine. He had flown it for three years over the Chaco, and it had not made a cough. Paul was thankful for that at least.

Now to get this thing off the ground. Paul's hands were sweating now, for he knew that on the six-hundred-foot strip at Asoe, absolutely nothing could go wrong on takeoff. The airplane must, must fly before six hundred feet passed beneath the wheels. That was barely enough distance to gather their needed speed. Once he was airborne, there were another six hundred feet of corridor in which Fucelli had cut down the taller trees, and Paul could level off over it to gain additional speed before climbing. He knew that, with the air this afternoon hot and thin, he would probably need it. He completed his takeoff check, setting the trim control, fuel boost, fuel valve, and wing flaps. They were ready to go.

There are several methods of getting an airplane off the ground in the shortest possible distance. Paul's favorite was to open the throttle wide with the brakes locked. The engine surged to twenty-six hundred revolutions per minute, and the motionless airplane shivered and screamed at being thus treated. Yes, it was an abuse of the engine, but it was not as bad as flying it through a tree. He then released the brakes, and the seat gave him a satisfying kick in the back as the DeVoss surged ahead. Holding the tail down, he steered with the tailwheel against engine torque, which, unchecked, would carry them off the airstrip. The controls came alive, and he nudged the wheel forward, raising the tail, steering with his rudder in the passing slipstream. The jungle of Cardinioso sped by on both sides with increasing speed. At the midpoint of the runway, there was a red tag tied to a stake; if their airspeed did not reach at least forty miles an hour before passing this marker, Paul would abort the takeoff. The decision must be made in a millisecond. A flash of red blurred by the wing. *Yes, go!* They were committed to the takeoff; there could be no successful stop now.

Marilyn and the Indians flashed past the wing, waving. Looking over Paul's shoulder from the jump seat, Fucelli was hypnotized by the quinee pede trees rushing toward them in the windshield. *Fifty, fifty-five*—Paul nudged the wheel back, and *Eighty-six Zulu*, with its light load of fuel, rose skyward with room to spare. Roaring into the corridor, now, with the quebracho trees flowing by on both sides, Paul held the nose level. *Let her pick up speed.*

"Oh, Lord," Fucelli breathed. The trees ahead were coming right at them.

Sixty-five, seventy. They had it made now,

thin air or not. Paul pulled back the wheel, feeling through his controls the satisfyingly solid slipstream as the DeVoss ballooned skyward like a shot. Fucelli watched the grasping trees fall suddenly far below them. They were free, climbing into an open sky.

This used to be a moment of pure happiness for Paul when, on a short-field takeoff, he would gather more than enough speed and then rocket upward, giving the illusion he really was invincible in the air. Lately, though, the feeling had eluded him.

At mission headquarters in Colonia, Alfredo Savillas paced the radio-room floor and paused at the window to watch the threatening sky to the south. "A fast-moving, narrow warm front," the weather station at Puerto Sastre confirmed. It rolled across the flat landscape like an aerial steam roller, billowing rolling cumuli in an unbroken line and leaving beneath it the greenish black of torrential rain, wind, and hail. Savillas watched it slowly engulf the southern end of Viejo Montana, the timbered ridge that jutted from the table-flat land just southwest of Colonia. The wind puffed his black hair as the first heavy drops splattered in. He lowered the glass, his handsome Spanish features dark with concern. *Why won't Paul Graham answer his radio?* he thought. *He must be in the air by now. What on earth could keep him at Asoe?*

Savillas strode to the radio to call again. "Colonia base calling *Eighty-six Zulu*. Paulo? Colonia base standing by for *Eighty-six Zulu*. Please reply."

There was no answer from Paul; instead the husky voice of Marilyn Fucella came over the speaker. "Asoe station to Colonia base. Is that you, Senor Savillas? Over."

"Yes, yes. Where is Graham? Over."

"Ed and Paul just took off in the plane a few minutes ago. They're bringing the chief's son to Colonia, to the clinic. They should certainly be able to hear us—"

There was another long moment of silence, and Savillas turned his eyes upward, imploring. "Paulo, perhaps you can hear me," he said into the microphone. "Listen, there is plenty of fuel at Bahia Negra if you must fly over there to refuel. Also, there is a very violent storm front moving through Colonia now. It isn't likely you can reach here, Paulo. Filadelfia will be clear for a short time. You should try there. Over."

"The hospital at Filadelfia will do fine," Marilyn said.

Another disquieting pause followed. "The weather here is beautiful," Marilyn said plaintively. "What's the matter? The airplane sounded all right when it took off. I'm sure nothing—"

"I'm sure it is only that Paulo's radio has malfunctioned once more," Savillas said. "Perhaps it will break on again soon. I will continue calling them."

Paul checked the circuit breaker and reached under the instrument panel to pound his Judas radio. "What a time to go dead! Of all the stinking luck!"

From over his pilot's shoulder, Fucelli watched this display of frustration, wondering why Paul was so upset over a trivial matter. After all, the big hurdle had been crossed, had it not? They were in the air. They would soon have Campemai safely in the hands of Dr. Brubacher in Colonia. The missionary soon learned, however, that the matter was more than trivial.

"We can't refuel," Paul called back over the engine's roar, as he snapped the microphone harshly back into its holder.

"Why not?"

"If we fly to Bahia, and they don't have any gas, we'll be stuck on the ground there for a week! And there's no way we can learn if they have any. Alfredo was supposed to find out for me. Now we can't contact him."

Fucelli stared at the back of his pilot's head silently. This wasn't according to Hoyle. When the patient is aboard the rescue plane, all problems are supposed to be over. He felt vaguely cheated. "Now what?" he shouted.

Paul did not answer at first, for he was fighting the temptation to turn around and land at Asoe and use the shortwave there to contact Savillas. But that would take time, time they did not have. And fuel that could well be irreplaceable.

"OK," he tried to grin back at Fucelli. "We'll just have to fly on to Colonia. My schoolboy arithmetic says we can make it if we take a few precautions."

Precautions, he thought wryly. *Sure.* They would have to wring every iota of flying time from the fuel they had. Grimly he leaned out the fuel mixture and adjusted the propeller into a coarser pitch, decreasing the engine speed. The cylinder-head temperature began to rise immediately. Here was another abuse of the engine. But if they were to reach Colonia with any margin of safety at all, there was simply no other choice. "Maybe the wind will give us a break, huh?" he called back.

Fucelli agreed, for the prospect of a flight over this endless jungle with dwindling fuel was quite uninviting. "We should pray for a tailwind if it's that critical," he shouted.

Paul did not reply. Fucelli could pray, certainly. But as for Paul, it had been a long time since he had talked to his Lord in prayer, and he did not feel he should try it now. He grimaced. That was funny: a missionary pilot who could not pray.

"I remember you said you had saved enough money to buy a new radio," Fucelli shouted. "What happened?"

The question caught Paul off guard, but he tried to conceal it. "It's a long story," he said finally. "I'll tell you later, OK?"

The little missionary shrugged and busied himself with checking Campemai's pulse, and Paul Graham was left alone with his miserable thoughts. Yes, it was a long story. The money donated to him by Christians back home was not going to buy a new radio, as they had supposed, but would instead be used for a quite different purpose. Paul sighed. He had known of a few missionaries who had been defeated, who had grown disillusioned and left the field in bitterness, conquered. But it always happened to others; it would never happen to him and Nancy. And Paul still could not believe it indeed had. Nancy's bitterness against the Lord and the unraveling of his own nerve and faith had taken their toll during the months since Eddy's death.

And then, as if this were not enough, it seemed that Satan was weaving a web to defeat them totally. His aircraft radio had begun to malfunction at the worst possible time. Such a problem sounded trivial, but it could be maddening, and one evening Nancy's pent up feelings had burst out in the now cheerless adobe house on Calle Palma. "It wouldn't have been so bad today if I had only known you were all right!" she had said vehemently. "If that stupid radio quits again, I don't know what I'll do."

"Everything's stupid this evening," he had grinned.

"It certainly is! Paul, you don't understand what I went through waiting for you. I don't think you understand at all. When you didn't answer anymore, I didn't know if you'd gone down, or what. We—we've already lost our son; now I'm supposed to cheerfully give you up, too?"

"Just what am I supposed to do, Nancy?" Paul was on the defensive, and he did not like it. "Alfredo and I are trying to fix the radio. What else can we do? Just give it the right combination of heat and vibration, or what have you, and it conks out. Let it cool down, and it works just fine. How can you fix something like that?"

"You can buy a new one. That's how you can fix it!"

"That's thirteen hundred dollars, honey. You know we don't have that. And the engine is coming due for a major overhaul in a few months."

Nancy's slender hands trembled. "Do you see what I've been telling you? Here we are, we can't even afford decent equipment. I mean, if people don't think this mission is important enough to send enough money, it's crazy for you to risk your life."

"I'm not risking my life!" he snapped.

"You are! If you ever went down in that Godforsaken mess, do you think we could ever find you? I'm not that naive."

Thus it was that the next issue of Interior Evangelism's newsletter had carried the following item: "Emergency prayer request for Paul and Nancy Graham, Colonia, Paraguay. Experiencing extreme difficulties following accidental death of their four-year-old son. Also needed: $1400 to purchase new shortwave for mission aircraft based at Colonia, flown by Paul Graham. Urgently needed for flight safety over uninhabited areas."

Assurances of prayer and sympathy began to arrive in the Mission's postbox in Asunción, and with surprising speed, money for the needed radio began to build in the Grahams' account.

But Satan was not to be outmaneuvered, nor was his web to be broken easily. Another kind of letter arrived in this mail of encouragement, postmarked Catawba, Virginia, from Nancy's parents. "Admitting a mistake," the letter read, "isn't easy, we know. But, Nancy, your Father and I are sure you've realized your mistake now, and we want you to know we understand. Dad and I have talked it over, honey, and if you and Paul want to come home, we have a place for you. Your Dad is reaching the age where this farm is too much for him, and we have decided to give you and Paul the south three hundred acres. You could cut a driveway in from the Blacksburg road and build your house on that grassy hill, or in the trees. And we know that Paul would do well with cattle and timber. . . ."

Nancy cried, then laughed. "Oh, Paul, think of that!" Her oval eyes shone for the first time in months. "Think of having a house! Think of having a house on that hill and seeing the mountains again."

After two months of spiritual darkness, growing fear, and alienation from his wife, this offer, and Nancy's reaction to it, tipped the balance. The idea flowed over Paul Graham's spirit like a cooling breeze. Defeat was easy.

The day after this decision, Paul flew to Asunción to pick up Dr. Pearson, who, with typical heartiness, insisted they lunch together before the flight back. They chose a favorite sidewalk *confiteria* with shaded outdoor tables. From inside drifted the Paraguayan music of lyrical Guarani with harp and guitars. It was a haunting, sweet harmony that Paul associated with this land alone. Why was it, he wondered, that every time he sat down to eat with Pearson, music was wafting from somewhere? But it was fitting, for the old missionary had given so much on this continent, even his eyesight. Paul could not look into his fading eyes now, and instead he watched one of Asunción's old trolleys far down on the Avenida Lopez, as he uttered the hardest words of his life. "Travis, Nancy and I will be leaving in two weeks, at the end of the month. We're quitting."

The words fell to the table and lay there. Pearson looked up, mildly incredulous, as if Paul had just told a stale joke, then went back to cutting the beef. His voice, when he spoke, was quite tired. "You know? I'd been hoping I wouldn't hear that. What will you do, Paul?"

"Oh," Paul took a deep breath, "Nancy's parents have offered us three hundred acres to farm. It—it sounds pretty good. Nancy has always liked the idea of that."

"So instead of harvesting human souls, you'll be harvesting alfalfa and corn, eh? A poor return for the investment of your life, don't you think?"

Pearson, please! Don't turn the dagger in my heart.

But Travis Pearson could be ruthless at times. "I suppose you've convinced yourself this is God's will?"

Paul knew it was not God's will, and he did not particularly care. His anger rose. "Travis, it's a matter of saving my marriage and maybe my sanity! Haven't you noticed the shape I've been in lately? You should keep closer tabs on your personnel!"

Pearson sighed. "I'm not breaking a confidence here, but Savillas has talked to me about a small problem you seem to be developing with your flying."

Paul laughed harshly. "A small problem!"

"And certainly not a unique one. According to Savillas, it's quite common for pilots who've flown for years under semihazardous conditions. They begin to worry about the law of averages, you know—how much longer before it catches up with them. He believes it was triggered by Eddy's being killed."

"Why talk to Savillas and not me?"

"If you knew you were being observed, it would aggravate the situation, would it not? As it is, we've both been watching you." An edge crept into Pearson's voice. "I don't recommend quitting, Paul. Perhaps an early furlough, a good rest. But don't quit, for your sake, because probably you'll never come back. Will you and Nancy come over tonight, and we will pray about your decision?"

"No. It's too late for that. We've enough money in our support account to get back home and ship our stuff. I'll fly for you two more weeks, and maybe you can have a replacement by then."

"Money in your account? That money was donated for a new shortwave, if my memory is correct!"

"It's money donated in our name, for our use, Travis. Maybe your next pilot can buy the radio."

5

Of the Here and Hereafter

As Paul Graham, Ed Fucelli, and Campemai flew on, isolated by their dead radio, Savillas, in the radio room at Colonia, watched rain flow in sheets down the windows and tried to convince himself there was really no cause yet for alarm. Outside, the whining growl of Dr. Brubacher's Citroen approached the house, a car door slammed, and the engine revved and pulled away.

Brubacher must've given Pearson a lift from the clinic, Savillas guessed. Moments passed, and no one entered the house. *Maybe Pearson has forgotten something and must ride back*, Savillas thought. The old man's careful footsteps sounded across the veranda, and he entered, his clothes drenched, his white hair plastered down as though he had fallen into a pool of water.

"Travis, I thought you'd returned to the clinic! Why were you so long in the rain?"

Pearson was plainly angry with himself. "I thought Ernst had let me out on the far side of the house. I was mistaken—wasn't paying attention." Disgustedly he surveyed his wet clothes. "What a mess! I'll go up and change clothes now, for Brubacher will be back shortly. We must review some cost estimates together for our outstation clinics."

Shoulders back, Pearson stalked upstairs, leaving a perplexed Savillas. *How on earth could Travis become lost outside his own house?* Unless—yes, the old missionary could see very little in dim light, Savillas knew, and outside things were quite dark beneath the clouds and heavy rain. But Savillas had never known anything like this to happen, and it was a strangely subdued Pearson who came down the stairs a few minutes later.

"How is Ijomejene?" Savillas asked quickly, trying to turn the impending conversation away from Pearson's embarrassing experience.

"Her child, you mean? Not well at all, I'm afraid." He looked around the radio room. "Where is Nancy?"

"She must be sleeping yet. Last night was a long one for her at the clinic with Ijomejene, eh?"

"Apparently so! Well, I hope the girl is all right. I'll have Margaret check on her when school is dismissed. Now for the next question, where are Paul and Campemai?"

Savillas looked directly at Pearson. "We don't know. His radio must have conked out again,

Travis. Marilyn said they took off from Asoe a few minutes ago—Paul, Ed, and Campemai." Quickly he briefed Pearson on the developing situation. He told him about the dead radio that made them unable to inform Paul of the fuel available at Bahia or the fast-moving storm front rolling across his flight path.

Pearson, thoughtfully alert now, having forgotten his own trouble, stared closely for a moment at the huge Chaco map above the radio. "We can be reasonably sure that Paul will land at Bahia, can't we? He must have fuel. When he lands there, he'll call us on the radio there."

"I—I'm not certain, Travis. The last contact I had with him was as he approached Asoe; then he had about twenty-four gallons in his tanks."

"Is that enough fuel to reach here? Would you try it?"

Savillas hedged. "Paulo knows his airplane much better than I, and he is familiar also with the current winds aloft. I cannot guess his decision."

"Well, if he doesn't detour to Bahia, then he is probably flying—"

"Directly toward this storm," Savillas said.

Pearson swallowed hard. "What are his chances—no, certainly there is no way he could get through a storm this violent."

And this time Savillas did not hedge. "No, Senor. It would be quite suicidal. But, Travis, Paulo will see the clouds far ahead. He will make a decision based upon his fuel supply and location. We will simply have to trust him."

"But can we trust him?" Pearson asked sharply, and the glance between the two men told of long conversations together about what was happening to Paul Graham, to his nerve and ability. "But I suppose right now we must trust him. We must assume he is flying toward Bahia. What else can we do? When he lands there, we'll instruct him to avoid this weather system. He must arrange through Brazilian customs there to fly our Indian to a hospital—probably to Corumba—wouldn't you think?"

"I like that, yes. It would be much better than flying this direction. The clinic at Filadelfia will probably be closed behind the storm soon also. It will be better if he doesn't fly this direction at all."

The two men were silent then, and Pearson stared blankly at the rain-washed window. "I pray he is going to Bahia," he said at length. "So much is at stake in this flight. So much. I wish Ed hadn't gone with them, you know? There is too much at stake as it is."

"What was it you called Fucelli once?" Savillas smiled. "A choice—"

"A choice spirit," Pearson said. "There are few men who could equal Ed's work at Asoe. He is God's man for that tribe, and, in my opinion, he is irreplaceable."

"Then certainly we can depend on God to care for him and them all, can we not?"

Pearson's infectious smile lit his face briefly. "Yes, yes. I think I was forgetting that. You know, Alfredo, have I ever told you of how Ed found Christ and how he joined our Mission?"

Without waiting for a reply, Pearson sank into a chair beside the radio and, perhaps to relieve his own tension, told the story of Ed Fucelli. He was a petty crook, a bookie, who managed his own bar in Muncie, Indiana. The bar was a convenient place for men to place bets, drink and fight, and meet with other men's wives. By day he drank and slept, and by night he ran his bar. "I was getting to be like a cockroach hiding under a trash can," he later said. "Afraid of the light."

But one day the light barged in on him anyway, in the form of a street evangelist, the type of preacher respectable people shun and the newspapers subtly deride. But this preacher knew his Lord, and he led a repentant and sobbing Fucelli to Jesus Christ that day. "His Christian faith took root and grew phenomenally," Pearson laughed. "And I shall always thank the Lord for calling Ed into mission work, and for leading him to us."

"He is one that people would least expect to be a missionary."

"True. You know, I'll never forget the time we all stopped at Quitaque. There was Ed Fucelli and Ed McCoy, Smith the pilot, and myself all standing in the little storehouse there. And two of McCoy's Indians began to fight over some disagreement, right there in front of the counter. I tell you, Alfredo, it looked bad for a moment. They were both muscular fellows and squared off with their lances there. I had no intention of interfering with them. And then, so quickly I could barely follow it, Fucelli jumped over the counter with a bottle of molasses in his hand and tapped the closest Indian directly at the base of his skull. Just a light tap like this," Pearson demonstrated. "And the Indian's legs simply buckled. The other fellow was so surprised he ran from the storehouse, and there we were, all gaping at Ed, almost as stunned as the Indian on the floor. And Ed just grinned back and said, "I must be out of practice. Usually I can get both of them!"

Savillas laughed. "Indeed, a choice spirit!"

"It was then I knew Fucelli was our man for the Edigo tribe," Pearson said. He paced to the window and looked out for a moment again. "I declare, Alfredo, I can't escape the feeling something is dreadfully wrong. If they're in danger, you know, it is partially my doing. I should have grounded Paul two weeks ago, after that day in Asunción. And that plane, too, shouldn't be flying with a defective radio. I should never have allowed Paul to continue without fixing that radio or arranging to procure another one in some way." He sighed audibly. "That was a bad decision. I'm getting too old for this job, Alfredo.

Like our airplane, I'm becoming old, and the different parts are beginning to wear out."

Surprised that the despairing mood had come so quickly over Pearson, Savillas shifted uncomfortably in his chair. It seemed, perhaps because of his soulful, dark eyes, that people always confided in him, and he found it mildly annoying during those times when he was unable really to help them. So he chuckled. "Travis, a few moments ago you became disoriented in the darkness outside. And now you are worried, perhaps needlessly, over Paul's flight. And because of this, you are forgetting the excellent job you are really doing here. Shame on you."

"Savillas, you are a positive tonic," Pearson smiled. "I appreciate the compliment. But seriously, we both know my days at this post are growing short. Before long, I will need someone to lead me by the hand when I am in Asuncion on business, and that is the day I must hang up the gloves, so to speak. And, Alfredo, I resent it! I'm not nearly ready to retire from this job. Just this morning I read from 2 Timothy 4:6-8 the apostle Paul's farewell remarks written before his execution." Pearson quoted from memory, "'The time of my departure is at hand. I have fought a good fight, I have finished my course, I have kept the faith: henceforth there is laid up for me a crown of righteousness, which the Lord, the righteous judge, shall give me at that day: and not to me only, but unto all them also that love his appearing.'

"When the apostle wrote those words, he knew his life was nearly over, that his job was done. But my job isn't done, not nearly so. Ernst Brubacher and I are finalizing plans for the outstation clinics—he should be here momentarily with some cost estimates—and there are the schools—"

The clinics, Savillas knew, were a project close to Pearson's heart. To provide basic medical care for his Indians, for their numerous tribal ills and accidents. A good deal of air-ambulance travel could be avoided, and the clinics would demonstrate that God is love and that He cares for the body as well as the soul. Pearson had plans also for schools to teach Indians in each tribe to read their own language. He was of the firm opinion that no one could really grow in the Christian life unless he could absorb God's Word daily. So, of course, a man must be able to read, and Scripture must be translated for him into his own language.

"Our anthropologist friends sometimes disagree with me on these things," Pearson would often laugh. "But they see the Indians as scientific specimens, while I see them as human beings with souls, spirits, and feelings like anyone else."

"So it is an old dog's trick," Pearson went on, "to begin these projects. My successor will be morally bound to complete them when I'm gone. But I have no desire to go, to retire. Ernst says that when I retire, I will at last have time to perfect my chess game." Pearson chuckled briefly. "But I ask, how can a blind man play chess?"

"The Lord has blessed you with a great memory," Savillas ventured.

"Yes, and I praise Him for it. I shall be needing it."

"The Lord has blessed you in many other ways as well, Travis. You've had a good life of service to Him, and your life has purpose. You fret for your goals, not yet completed, and yet most men have never had goals at all, except their own self-indulgence. I see it more and more in my clients, the hunters I fly deep into the wilderness. Out where there is so much to know and see—even there they must soothe their minds with whiskey. Why? Because they are so empty within, as desperately empty as I was." Savillas gestured with a big hand over his chest. "They have no purpose, and their work has no lasting consequence, if any. So see how fortunate you are. You have served God the whole of your life and have yet to exhaust the challenge of it. Your work will be rewarded through eternity, for the Indians who have found Christ through this mission will be there to bless you. You are most fortunate of all men."

"Henceforth there is laid up for me a crown of

righteousness," Pearson murmured softly. "Thank you, Alfredo, for reminding me of some basic things. But, you know, I haven't done it for a reward. It's just that I love Him so, my Saviour."

"And perhaps that is why your people love you as they do."

Pearson smiled. "And you know, possibly it isn't the Lord's will for me to continue here indefinitely, after all. Perhaps if a younger, more forceful man had been here, Paul and Ed wouldn't be in the impending danger they're in."

Pearson returned to the radio and sat down. They listened a moment to the wind-driven rain roaring against the glass. "Alfredo," Pearson said thoughtfully, "sometimes we do things, and we wonder why we did them. And I think now, after becoming lost in the rain as I did, and after this talk we've had, I see now why I've allowed Paul to continue flying. You see, I'm afraid of change now. I want everything to continue just as it is, with the same people, Paul and Nancy, the Fucellis, and all the others. I want us all to continue just as we are, serving the Lord together. Because if anything changes, if anyone should leave, it would force me to acknowledge that things do indeed change, and that one day soon, I must leave as well. Do you understand what I'm trying to say?"

"I believe I do, yes," said Savillas.

"You'll understand better when you become old," said Pearson. "And so I desperately wanted Paul and Nancy to continue with us, and, against my better judgement, I let him keep flying, hoping that this spiritual sickness would pass. Now," the old man took a deep breath, and his voice trembled slightly, "I simply can't escape this feeling that today we will pay for my mistaken decision."

Savillas was becoming annoyed now, but he tried to conceal it. One would think this was the first storm the sky had ever known, or that Paul had begun flying only yesterday.

At that moment Ernst Brubacher entered the house. The doctor, as much a feature of Colonia as the cheese produced there, carried a briefcase in place of his usual medical bag, and Pearson rose abruptly to meet him. "Look," he told Savillas, "tell me as soon as you contact Graham. We'll divert him up to Corumbá if we can." Pearson showed the doctor to his office.

"Now remember, Travis," Ernst Brubacher boomed, "I'll not let you capture my nurse!"

"You sound as though we're playing chess, Doctor."

Their laughter faded behind the closed door, and Savillas began again to call Bahia Negra, wondering in which direction Paul was headed and what thoughts were going through his mind at this moment.

Campemai's moans were growing noticeably weaker, and it seemed to Fucelli that the plane was hanging motionless in the sky, getting nowhere. He thrust his bald head between the seats. "How much longer, Paul?"

"About a hundred more miles, Fudd. I figure maybe forty-five minutes. We'll be passing over the *Riacho Obelebit* in a minute, and then I can tell you exactly." Paul needed a definite landmark to determine their groundspeed, for as they flew farther southeast, the land below them was becoming green and swampy, crisscrossed with small tributaries of the Rio Paraguai. Through this sea of jungle treetops shimmered the *Riacho,* a perfect landmark, except that a pilot had to be directly over it before it was visible to him through the trees.

With his now characteristic nervousness, Paul began looking for it long before he should. It was a good thing, too. The river, now darkened in evening shadows, rolled into view ten minutes ahead of schedule! This was too good to be true. The knot in his stomach suddenly easing, Paul dialed their time en route on the disk of the Jeppesen computer and read out a new groundspeed of 165 miles an hour.

"Hey, Fudd! The wind's not as strong as I thought. At this speed, we'll be there in thirty minutes! We might even have some gas left over. How's that?"

"Thank the Lord." Fucelli grinned.

Paul permitted himself a tight smile. The foreboding darkening his mind since the beginning of this flight—how foolish it suddenly seemed. This flight would end routinely, like all the others. Then he would make one or two more. He would fly Fucelli back to Asoe and perhaps make one more supply run, then he and Nancy would leave for the States. But the thought brought him no happiness, and he was glad Fucelli didn't know of his plans of betrayal.

So they flew on. Even though Paul kept the fuel mixture lean and the revolutions per minute low, the cylinder head temperature stayed within tolerable limits as the engine squeezed every ounce of energy from their fuel. Yes, they would make it fine. Even the thunderheads billowing from the horizon did not at first alarm Paul. They must be the storms Savillas had mentioned in his last radio contact. Local thunderstorms no doubt, and they would present no problem unless one happened to be sitting right over the airfield. Otherwise, Paul would simply detour around them, since his fuel supply was now adequate to do so. Nevertheless, he watched them warily as a wild stallion would survey the ominous, encircling gauchos.

Moments passed. As the clouds rose higher into view above the earth's curvature, Paul realized they were not the isolated storms he had at first supposed. His eyes strained, peering through sixty miles of atmosphere. Yes, they were towering columns rising from what appeared to be an unbroken line of low cumuli billowing directly from the horizon. It seemed to extend as far east as he could see, and it dissolved into the southwest haze in an unbroken barrier. *A front?*

Instinctively he seized the microphone. He must learn if this was indeed a weather front, spawned by the forces of high and low pressure playing through the atmospheric ocean. Savillas must tell him if Colonia was clear and how far south this barrier of storm and cloud extended.

Just as quickly he remembered that the radio was not functioning, but he tried anyway, calling Colonia again and again, changing bands to call Puerto Sastre and Filadelfia. He banged on the radio and checked the circuit breaker for the nth time. But his cries were swallowed in the endless sky, and no answer returned. Irritably he snapped the useless microphone back into its clip.

Of course! He remembered his vague premonition. Now he began to see from whence it came. His subconscious had suspected it all along. Like a web to snare him, it had all come together: his low fuel, his wounded passenger near death, the prospect of a tribal war if he died, the weather front boiling far ahead, and now a dead radio when he desperately needed to know what was beyond those clouds.

So, Paul, you think you'll quit so easily? You

think you'll misuse money given by hard-working Christians at home? They gave it to buy a new radio to advance the Christian message, and you reserved it instead to finance your own miserable retreat. Did you think you'd get away with that?

Fucelli slid up front again to see Paul sweating, wiping moist hands on his trousers, his lips trembling slightly. He sensed immediately the seemingly tangible fear. What was wrong? Only a moment ago they had been cheering their excellent groundspeed. "What's up, buddy?"

"I—oh man, Fudd," Paul pointed silently toward the horizon. Fucelli gazed out at the line of white clouds far ahead, rolling from the horizon with darkness beneath them. At intervals, high columns boiled skyward like pictures he had seen of atomic mushroom clouds.

"That's about fifty miles ahead. It's right between us and Colonia," Paul shouted.

"Can we still get there?"

Paul took a deep breath. "I don't know yet. I have no idea how thick it is. I don't know what's on the other side, if Colonia is clear, or what!"

Fucelli's heart sank. What did Paul mean, he didn't know? They had to reach Colonia; didn't he realize that? "What can we do?" Fucelli asked sharply, his eyes suddenly smoldering.

"I don't—don't know." Paul shook his head like a man recovering from a knockout punch. *Think, man!* A knot clutched his entrails. His brain was so fogged that he was forgetting the very basics of piloting. Painfully, he forced his mind to function. Like a beleaguered businessman he must add his assets and liabilities against projections for the immediate future, but in Paul's case, failure would be much more disastrous than bankruptcy. His assets were very few. Both gasoline gauges hovered between one-quarter and empty—there were about eight gallons in each wing. So, the engine could run for another hour at the most. That was enough time to reach Colonia if they flew straight through the storms.

As for liabilities, he had already reviewed them, and they were staggering. Adding to their difficulties, sunset was due in another hour, and the short, subtropical twilight would fade quickly. *But what of it?* Paul thought morbidly. With the engine due to quit before then, the fact that it would soon be dark was immaterial. If he flew through what was now obviously a front—

Paul knew that those boiling clouds possessed the kinetic energy of an atomic bomb. Cells of turbulence, high-speed air currents shearing against one another, would turn *Eighty-six Zulu* into a spinning piece of wreckage in seconds. He was not fooling himself. He would not penetrate that front and commit suicide.

"Fudd, do you know if there's another doctor within a hundred miles of here?"

"Doctor?" the missionary shouted. "Paul, we need a surgeon, a hospital. You know that!"

Paul, with hopelessness forming like lead in his stomach, scanned the aerial chart. Obviously there was only one other hospital in range of his fuel. That was the Mennonite clinic at Filadelfia, about one hundred miles southwest.

Fucelli, eyeing the chart over his shoulder, seemed to read his mind. "How about Filadelfia?"

"If we knew it was in the clear. If I could only talk to somebody on this lousy radio!"

"Where else can we go, Paul?"

Paul peered westward to where the frontal line disappeared into sunlit haze. He could see less than twenty miles in this direction. Maybe Filadelfia was clear, maybe not. "All right," he shouted as he swung the plane's nose southwest toward the low sun, "here's what we'll do, Fudd." He ran a finger across the chart, no longer caring if Fucelli saw its trembling. "See this dirt road—runs north from the Puerto Casada rail line toward Fortin Lopez. I'm going to aim for where the road intersects the rail line, right here. We should be able to tell from there if Filadelfia is open enough to land. We should be over that road in about—" He turned the Jeppesen's scale, then angrily punched the rudder pedals to bring the DeVoss back on course. *Blasted ship! Take your eyes off the compass for a second and it drifts left, wanders all over the sky.* His next plane would have rudder trim. *But there won't be a next plane, remember?* "OK", he said finally, "we should be over the road in twenty minutes, and we'll make our decision then. If we can't land at Filadelfia—we'll just have to land at Paso Moro and let Campemai take his chances."

"Take his chances!" Fucelli's jaw shot out. "You mean die, don't you?"

"Use your head, Fudd. We can't fly through a front!"

"We can at least try, can't we?" Fucelli could not believe that Paul would give up without even an attempt. "Paul, if we take Campemai back dead, do you know what'll happen?"

"I know," Paul snapped. "I was there, remember? You should've thought of this before you promised to save his life."

"I didn't promise—" Fucelli saw where the argument was headed and tried to quiet himself. "It's too late for hindsight now, isn't it?" he rasped finally.

Yes, it was too late, and the men flew on in wretched silence. Their course, diagonal to the storms, drew them closer to the majestic clouds looming above their tiny plane, orange in the sinking sun. Paul's eyes bored holes through the windshield, trying to penetrate the sun-yellowed haze, as he looked below for the road to Fortin Lopez and at the same time kept an eye on the clouds to the left.

Suppose, just suppose, he was crazy enough to

fly through them. What was the best way to do it? Punching straight through was out of the question, for, lacking the weather radar of larger planes, he could easily blunder into invisible cells of turbulence. Flying under the clouds offered a better possibility. But never had Paul seen such a violent front that, from his altitude of three thousand feet, appeared to be rolling literally across the ground. He must descend to at least five hundred feet to get under it. And then, flying blind through rain and hail, how easily he could be knocked out of control, slammed downward to vanish forever into the writhing, wind-blasted, jungle treetops. No, he wouldn't go under it. There was a third possibility. He could climb to about ten thousand feet and dodge between the towering columns. But that, too, was ridiculous. With his limited fuel, it was insane to be caught on top of a cloud mass the extent of which was unknown to him. There simply was no way, whether Fudd could understand it or not. There was no way.

Paul dreaded the moment when the junction of railroad and dirt track would come into view, for it was obvious the front extended far beyond them. The coming decision seemed to weigh on his soul, suffocating, and his hands trembled the more. Relentlessly, it came. In a few minutes they picked out the joining of the two narrow clearings snaking through the green sea below, with a miniature freight shack at the junction. As

Paul had feared, clouds had curved in front of them by now and were blocking out the sun, and the dark curtain of rain told both men Filadelfia was out of reach behind the storms.

Well, that was that; their last hope of reaching a surgeon was gone. Paul began a slow turn to the right, where he would follow the road to Paso Moro and land there. He could scarcely breathe. "Lord," he prayed ridiculously, "I'm sorry. You know I tried."

"Where are you going?" The words came low and stern from Fucelli, his eyes glowing with an inner intensity.

Paul could not look him in the face but pointed to the chart. "Right here. We'll land there."

"You mean there's no way we can get to either hospital? Are you telling me there's no way at all?"

"Ed, believe me—"

"No, I don't believe you! I don't trust you! You've been shaking like a reed ever since we saw the storm. What's wrong with you, Paul?"

Paul's trembling became almost convulsive. "Ed, it wouldn't do any good for us all to die," he pleaded.

"How many people will die at Asoe if we don't get this man to a surgeon? And you won't even try! You won't even try, you yellow *cobarde!* Don't tell me airplanes can't fly through storms!" Disgusted at the wretched sight of his pilot, he grasped Paul by the collar, pulling him sideways in an iron grip. "Paul, I swear, I oughta jerk you out of there and fly it myself!"

Paul's whole body shivered as if he had been slapped in the face. How fragile was the thread of rational thought that this sudden physical shock could break it; his mind seemed to clear, and the unbearable tension suddenly drained away. Both men stared dumbfounded at each other in the greenish twilight. Fucelli slowly released his grip as Paul, calmly, wordlessly, began a steady turn to the northeast.

"I'm sorry, Paul," Fucelli said, surprised at himself.

"Well, I guess we'll try it, Fudd." Paul smiled weakly. "I guess we'd better try if we want to keep living with ourselves, right?"

Fucelli smiled somewhat sheepishly and went back to the jump seat again. The iron-willed missionary did not realize what he had done; he didn't know the determination that had seized Paul Graham just then. Enough of cringing before fear, Paul thought. If he was going to waste the rest of his life farming in Catawba, he would at least do it knowing that, during his last week in Paraguay, he had saved a life and averted a tribal war. And if they failed to make it through the front—well, maybe it would be just as well. It was certainly better that than spending the rest of his life unable to bear his own cowardly company. Whether or not the Lord wanted him to challenge this storm, Paul did not know. And, as before, he did not care.

Colonia, he reasoned, since it was farther south, would probably clear before Filadelfia. He began a slow climb, his plane inching like a gnat across the face of a mammoth pink cloud, and settled the compass on a course for Colonia.

6

La Amaba Hasta Que Murio

As, high in the sky and far away, Paul Graham drew nearer his battle in the clouds, Nancy Graham awoke in their house on Calle Palma. She was aware of having slept for a very long time. Hovering in the twilight between consciousness and sleep, the slender girl couldn't tell how long. But it was so good to have slept soundly again, with no terror-filled dreams of Eddy to leave her crying and sweating in tangled bedsheets.

Then she remembered—yes, she had dreamed of him, a happy dream—he, running in the sun among the orange trees in their backyard. Paul had been in the dream, too. She sighed and reached out to him. How good to feel peace in her soul again, as thrilling as cool water on parched skin, and just as welcome. Where had it come from, this wonderful, unaccustomed peace?

Then the cold sheets on Paul's side of the bed reminded her that this was really evening of the day and he was not yet home. Not home? Her eyes opened suddenly in the bedroom's quiet twilight as she tried to orient herself, and the events of the previous evening swam into her sleep-logged memory. Of course. The happenings of that strange evening, they explained why Paul was not home. They explained, too, the new quiet of her soul. Still drowsy, she closed her eyes again to think them over.

It was early in the evening when Paul radioed that his propeller seals were leaking oil, and he must land at Fortin Coronel Varisca. Something else had gone wrong with that insufferable airplane; so what else was new?

After he was safely down at Varisca, she shut off the radio and went into Dr. Pearson's office to tell him what had happened. In the office with Pearson was a young missionary who had just completed deputation. One of Paul's last tasks with the mission would be to fly this young man out to Quitaque to spend the summer training with Ed McCoy. He was idealistic, fresh, and healthy. And, even though he knew Nancy would desert the mission in two more days, he still accorded her an annoying deference.

She flopped in a wicker chair and told Pearson about the leaking seals.

"What a shame it happened on your last two days here," he smiled. "Did Paul say he could fix them?"

"Oh yes, he talked like it would be no problem to fix. He'll be back tomorrow."

Pearson shook his head slowly. "That airplane. It's been nothing but trouble lately. You know, Nancy," he chuckled, "You and Paul have spent so much of your own support money on the plane, by rights it should be yours when you leave. Not that we could let you have it, of course."

"I would be glad never to see that airplane again," she said evenly.

"Yes, I suppose you would." Pearson, for all his usual cheer, looked quite worn. He and his wife had been taking turns spending nights at the clinic with Yocai's wife, Ijomejene, and her sick baby, and the strain was beginning to show. "You know," he said at length, "replacing your husband is going to be a difficult task."

For courtesy, Nancy feigned more interest than was genuine. "Didn't you say there's a boy interested in the job?"

"Oh, yes. I talked to him this morning, in fact, on the JAARS patch line. He graduates in two months but must complete his instrument training yet, and he still needs a great deal more deputation work to raise support. He can't be ready for another year at least."

Puente, sweating from exertion, ambled into the office then and playfully punched the new missionary's shoulder as he sank into the last available chair.

Pearson nodded a greeting and continued talking. "There are plenty of men who can fly, though not as many who can negotiate the short airstrips like Paul. And there are plenty of men licensed to repair airframes and powerplants, as they say. But men who can do both, and then will surrender this skill to the Lord for a fraction of their possible earnings in the commercial world, those men are hard to find. So, consequently, there's no one in sight just now to replace Paul. The JAARS fellows have agreed to fly our mail and supplies once a week. But if any emergency arises, we'll find ourselves in a tight place. We must abandon a few of our projects for awhile—"

"Like Ed McCoy's irrigation system at Quitaque," the alert young man cut in. "No pilot to fly in the equipment."

"Yes, that for one. Well," Pearson smiled directly at Nancy, "while Paul's resignation caught us relatively by surprise, I'm sure the Lord knew of it far in advance, and He will solve the problem in His own way. I hoped He would persuade you and Paul to stay on, but apparently He hasn't, eh?"

Nancy felt a rising discomfort. "Travis, you know I'm sorry. We've discussed all this before, and you know why Paul and I shouldn't be here any longer."

"Yes, yes. We've been through that. I can understand."

"I cannot!" Puente's gruff voice rumbled. It

was startling after Pearson's quiet speech. Nancy looked up but was unable to meet his direct gaze. "I cannot understand why anyone would forsake the Saviour, leave His service."

"Puente," Pearson cautioned, "Nancy is at a disadvantage—"

"And you, Dr. Pearson, are gentle, but you are too gentle. Why do you not rebuke her words when they are so baseless?"

"We can't say they're baseless."

"Absurdo. Certainly they are. Is not the Lord Jesus who saved my soul the same who can bring comfort to Nancy and Paulo? If only they would accept it! Nancy," he looked at her intensely, "I am sure. For what an impossible thing the Lord Jesus did for me, when he reached down and lifted me from hell!"

Nancy had heard before much of Puente's story, but never directly from him. He spoke with the light of wonder in his eyes. He was one who, as a young construction worker in Brazil, had fallen into that curious mixture of "Christianity" and voodoo prevalent there. Thirsting for peace, he would offer gifts to statues of the blessed virgin and the crucified Jesus, while with the same sincerity he worshiped Oxala and Iemanja, their voodoo counterparts. With a darkened face he told of the ritual dances and the horror of spirit communion, the voodoo ceremony that left his soul hungry and wretched. He described the tyranny of whiskey that ruined both his marriage and his employment.

This darkness of soul continued until one night, when as a charity patient in the Southern Baptist Hospital in Asunción, he discovered the living Jesus Christ. "I found Him in the pages of this Book." Puente pulled a New Testament from the pocket of his khaki shirt. "And for the rest of my life I will be grateful to the man who guided me there." The verses tumbled from his memory, "'While we were yet sinners, Christ died for us.'* 'He was buried, and . . . He rose again the third day'† 'If any man hear my voice and open the door, I will come in to him.'‡ This Jesus was the One for whom my soul cried," Puente said. "I opened the door to Him. I gave him my heart. And I found that He is not dead, hanging from a gold or an ivory cross. He is alive. He took the hunger for whiskey away from me." Puente's smile broadened. "Do you understand the words I've said? He took me from hell. And it is sure, Nancy, he can take you from the hell you have made for yourself."

"And you don't understand, Puente." Her voice hardened. "He took whiskey from you. From me He took the dearest thing I had, in a brutal, bloody way. I know the Bible says He loves me, but something inside has turned

---
*Romans 5:8
†Corinthians 15:4
‡Revelation 3:20

against Him, and I can't help it. It isn't my fault I can't love Him anymore!"

Puente rose to his feet. "Love? You are not one to speak of love!" Majestic in his sudden, righteous anger, he soared taller than all of them, and a surprised Pearson opened his mouth but did not speak. "You care nothing for anyone," Puente went on, "not even your husband. I have watched you killing your Senor Graham day by day."

"What are you talking about?" Nancy was near tears.

"I have watched the slow dying of his spirit within him because of you. You know he does not want to leave the Lord's work. He is content to leave now, yes, as a horse is content with a saddle—after his spirit has been broken!"

"That's quite enough!" Pearson said sharply.

Puente ignored him. "And I tell you more—Dr. Pearson is losing strength staying nights in the clinic. Not once have you offered help, because you care nothing for the Edigo or for anyone else. You know nothing of Jesus' love."

"That isn't true!" she said with surprising control and, marching past them, slammed the door of the office.

As she hurriedly left the house, she heard Pearson scolding, and Puente's reply, "Travis, the words needed to be said. You should have said them long ago."

That evening, alone in the silent house,

Puente's words would not leave her in peace: *You are killing your Senor Graham. You know nothing of Jesus' love.* Packing their clothes and dishes for shipment did not relieve her mind. On the shortwave she could find no good music, only religious programs on HCJB, which she did not want to hear. "All right!" she said finally, to no one in particular. "All right!" Anything to relieve the pressure on her soul! Through the warm twilight she walked to the airfield headquarters house, to find that Dr. Pearson had already gone. So back down Callé Unruh, past the large co-op store, to the one-story brick building which was the Colonia Clinic.

In the women's ward, the five iron beds were empty except one used by Ijomejene and, beside it, a crib with an intravenous bottle attached. Dr. Brubacher and his nurse were gone for the day, and a pleasantly startled Travis Pearson looked up from his Bible.

"I guess I can let you get a good night's sleep before I go," Nancy said.

"Well, God bless you," Pearson said softly. He reminded her to change the IV bottle, which she would do only once in the early-morning hours. And she was cautioned to watch the needle when Ijomejene moved the baby, and to check his temperature and breathing every so often. "I'll be going now, Nancy," he said. "And thank you again."

So the two women were left alone. Ijomejene, wearing a brightly colored Edigo skirt and one of Margaret Pearson's blouses, smiled shyly; the dimples in her wide face reminded Nancy of a cartoon chipmunk. Nancy judged her to be in her mid-twenties, which would make them about the same age, and apparently they were equally shy.

The first halting efforts at communication fared badly until Ijomejene suddenly began to laugh, apparently at Nancy's gestures or perhaps a linguistic *faux pas*. Nancy joined her, and they laughed together like two school girls. After that, further efforts revealed that each knew a little of the Guarani language, which Yocai must have taught his young wife. *He should've taught her more*, Nancy thought to herself. *But then, maybe he didn't want her to learn too much.* A phrase from the women's lib movement came to her mind, *the male chauvinist pig*.

Ijomejene, with no announcement, abandoned the language session for a while and began chewing a pear, which she spit into a cup. It was feeding time. With her own mouth she forced portions of the watery gruel through her child's lips, but the thin, brown baby refused to swallow and let it trickle down his cheek instead. He was slightly more interested in the milk, smacking his lips loudly at her breast. Nancy carefully guided the IV tube and, hearing the baby's satisfied gurgles, felt an old ache revive; Eddy had fed in the same way. In a moment, though, the boy stopped eating and began to stiffen and wail, perhaps from stomach pain. Obviously, he was not getting well. Ijomejene held him desperately close while tears welled in her dark almond eyes; the pathos of her face needed no language for expression.

"I know how you feel," Nancy said in English. "I know how you feel."

It came back to her then, like a flood. She remembered the first years when she had been enthusiastic and fresh like the young man in Pearson's office. She had flown with Paul to several of the mission stations then. The Indians? They were strange, naked, sometimes deformed ghosts of the forest. She could not speak their language, she held nothing in common with them, yet her heart burned to help them know her Saviour, to know the peace eluding them for eons. Somewhere that concern had been lost along the dark paths of her prodigal journey from the Lord. But now it was stirring to life again this soft summer night, given new birth by the face of Ijomejene, for how well Nancy knew the hurt in her eyes.

Later, after the baby's crying had subsided, a worn Ijomejene tried to tell Nancy of her baby lying emaciated in the crib. Language was not equal to the task, so with surprising skill, she drew a series of pictures on a yellow pad. The first sketch showed a crying baby being put in a grave, and Nancy was puzzled. Had one of Ijomejene's earlier children died? No, the Indian woman gestured. This was the same child. Then, in mock anger, she marked through the sketch. No, the baby was not buried because—she pointed toward the sky and then to her heart, and Nancy recognized the word *Jesus* in "*Jesus Uje-Chignorai.*"

The second picture was of the child lying in Paul's airplane. At last Nancy understood. Paul had told her that the Edigo valued healthy babies, but sickly ones were regarded as worthless and were often buried alive and forgotten. A chill ran through Nancy as she realized what would have been the fate of this baby were it not for *Jesus Uje-Chignorai*, who, Ijomejene said, was in her heart.

A warmth of joy began to rise in Nancy's soul. *Does Christ make a difference? Obviously so, and what a priceless treasure is found in knowing Him!* She felt tears coming but fought them back, for there had been too much crying this night already. But the corners of her mouth trembled as she pointed skyward, then to her own heart, telling Ijomejene that she too knew *Jesus Uje-Chignorai.*

These events paraded through Nancy's awakening mind now. Yes, the peace with which she had fallen asleep this morning was still with her. Perhaps this was why she had slept so long and soundly. Was there a chance she would stay in Paraguay now? Was there really anything on earth more important than carrying the message of Christ to everyone who would hear it? What a surprise for Paul if she told him she had changed her mind, that she wanted to stay! She chuckled at the thought, and her sleep-tendered heart ached for him, wanting to melt again in his embrace. Maybe they would have a quiet, candlelight dinner when he came home.

The small barrels in which she would pack the clothes, dishes, and Paul's treasured history books of this courageous little country, were still stacked on the floor in a silent rebuke. Was she too optimistic? The barrier of resentment she had built against God was so wide!

No, the tempter whispered, *a barrier that formidable can't be overcome so easily.* Overcoming it would require her complete surrender to God's will. Could she ever really do that again? Then, too, her dream of a house on the hill with a view of the mountains—her own house with her and Paul and the family they would raise on their farm—that dream would not die so easily, either.

How dark it was, and the air through the bedroom shutters was so warm! *It shouldn't be getting dark yet!* Suddenly, from the north, a rumble of thunder shook the land. Over the bedroom shutters she peered to see the northern sky black with massive clouds. The sky overhead was clear, and to the southwest, a shaft of sunlight lying on the horizon like molten gold cast an unworldly light over the earth. Wisps of ominous fog rose from the ground, soaked by the storm which had passed over without waking her. Where was Paul? Certainly he was nowhere near that storm! Her heart quickening, she switched on the shortwave receiver, hoping to catch some chatter between the stations while she dressed. Probably he was still at Varisca, or even at home. While tuning to the mission's band, from a station somewhere she caught the phrase of a popular song, *"La amaba hasta que murio"* ("He loved you till he died").

"Paul?" She shuddered with a sudden, unaccountable chill as her voice echoed in the silence. "Paul, no!" Quickly she put on her clothes and hurried up steaming Calle Palma toward the airfield.

7

In the Clouds Lies Eternity

They flew parallel to the billowing, white clouds, vaporous mountains in the sky, glowing now with a pink tinge from the setting sun. Paul Graham and Ed Fucelli sat awestricken at the majesty that dwarfed them to nothing. Their plane seemed to be only an insect crawling across the face of vast, rolling whiteness. They would reach Colonia, right or wrong, Paul decided, by going over the storms.

His strange calm still persisted; his thinking was now clear. A savage stab of pleasure pierced him as, glancing back at Fucelli, he saw that the missionary's face was calm. Obviously he trusted Paul in spite of the pilot's sorry performance a few moments ago. "What do you think?" Paul shouted over the roar of the engine.

Fucelli shook his head. "You're the pilot."

Yes, Paul was the pilot; the outcome of this flight was in his hands, and they were steady hands. But whether it was in God's hands or not, he was not sure. Certainly he would soon find out.

He swung south toward the storm and opened the throttle to begin a steady climb. The solid roll-cloud ahead, floor of this warm front, topped out at about six thousand feet; behind it rose the columnar, awesome thunderheads, scraping the stratosphere at thirty thousand. But there were gaps between these monsters, canyons and valleys through which Paul, at about ten thousand feet, could slip unscathed. This was the way they would cheat the elements. What a joke to slip over this holocaust without a drop of water hitting the windshield, without a bump in the air! He grinned back at Fucelli, "Well, we're flying over this mess, Fudd. What do you say to that?"

"We can do it?" Fucelli, who knew little about flying, seemed to doubt that this could be done.

"If we get high enough. We'll go between the thunderheads."

"You're the pilot," Fucelli said again.

The cylinder-head temperature rose dangerously in this full-throttle climb, and Paul slid the mixture knob forward to feed the engine a richer, cooler burning mixture. This gulped more fuel, of course, but it was useless to save fuel and burn out the engine. The fuel gauges registered near empty now; Paul scanned them and did not look again. *What,* he wondered, *would Savillas do in a situation like this? Nonsense. Even the flamboyant Savillas wouldn't try an insane stunt like this. A sensible pilot would not climb over an* overcast without knowing his destination was clear.

Without a working radio, Paul could not know this. Nor did he know how far south this front extended. What assurance did he have of adequate fuel to reach clear weather? None whatsoever. He was depending on sheer luck, and he knew it. If they were all killed, Savillas would probably wonder what had happened to Senor Graham's mind to try such a foolish thing. Or maybe, remembering their conversation in the jeep on Calle Palma, he would suspect—

A quavering moan rose from behind him, audible above the engine, and Paul exchanged a harried, backward glance with Fucelli. Whatever happened, he dared not climb above ten thousand feet, where the air becomes rapidly thinner and oxygen more scarce. Although he and Fucelli could tolerate it. Campemai probably could not. "Fudd," Paul called, "make sure Campemai is strapped in tight. We might bounce around a little. Then strap yourself in the jump seat real good."

Fucelli, as he knelt on the cargo floor, was glad to cease staring at those beautiful but horrible clouds. He felt as though if he did not look at them, they would go away. Thank God they were climbing and not descending into the blackness beneath the clouds! Psychologically, at least, going over the top was the better way.

The tough, corded missionary, still smoldering with shame at his temper of moments before, felt at peace with their decision. Campemai, gleaming with sweat, was weakening gradually, and, obviously, without a surgeon he would soon die. Besides, something in Paul's face spoke of no retreat; Fucelli could not back out now, even if he wanted to. Probably that was as it should be and 2 Corinthians 12:9 echoed in his heart: *"My strength is made perfect in weakness."* He prayed a short prayer for them all, especially for Paul. *O Lord, work thy will through him now, even though his will is so far from thine. Forgive us if we have presumed on thy mercy, Father. Don't let your plans fail because of our sin. Forgive me for my temper.*

At peace, Fucelli eased back into the jump seat and looked out at a scene of unbelievable beauty. The ground had disappeared. Paul had leveled out over a floor of pinkish, fluffy clouds, while on both sides, billowing, cumulus columns towered. They floated, a speck, through this giant cathedral in the sky. "Lord!" Fucelli breathed. Not a swear word, but an exclamation of genuine praise.

For Paul Graham, staring into the sides of his cloudy canyon, there were no words of praise but only a warning, written by a pioneer pilot of years ago "In the clouds lies eternity."

From the ground, thunderheads appear quite stable. But seen from the terrifying intimacy of *Eighty-six Zulu,* they were in constant motion, rolling and billowing like steam from a slow-motion geyser. Paul held the compass on 180 degrees, straight south toward Colonia, and wondered how long their canyon would continue. It was growing darker as they left the sun behind, and even as he wondered, the cloud floor seemed to begin rising toward him while the narrow hallway of dark blue sky ahead began to close. It was as if the giants of the air, angry at this noisy, intruding insect, were reaching down to pinch it in their obese fingers.

He considered climbing again, and from nowhere they were suddenly deluged in roaring, blinding rain like he had never experienced. The windshield became an opaque screen of frenzied, cascading water, and the engine's rumble was lost in the unearthly roar of an airborne waterfall. The tachometer quickly assured him, however, that the engine was still running. As he shifted his attention to flying blind on instruments, he pulled carburetor heat to prevent the venturis from icing up, for water in a thunderstorm can be very cold. He did not bother shouting back to reassure Fucelli, since the missionary could not hear him anyway. Obviously the rain was plunging down on them from one of the cumulus columns, and they would probably fly out of it in a few minutes.

Flying blind by instruments, a pilot must be quite narrow-minded, believing his instrument panel to the exclusion of all else. The airspeed indicator and control pressures convey his true airspeed to senses that may otherwise insist he is sitting still. Though he may feel he is turning, if the turn-and-bank indicator and steady compasses indicate the wings are level, he must believe them. The artificial horizon, vertical speed indicator, tachometer, and altimeter will all combine to tell if he is nosing up or down; he clings blindly to their advice, for deprived of vision, his own sense of up and down may become erratic.

Paul knew this principle, of course. He also knew its counterpart in the Christian life; a Christian must trust his Lord's Word to the exclusion of his own changeable senses. But he, like many Christians, found it difficult to apply.

They did not fly out of the rain, however. Quite suddenly it grew darker and the air became rough as the DeVoss began to balloon upward and plunge sickeningly, striking the solid aircurrents with teeth-rattling jolts. Thank the Lord, Fucelli thought, that they had tightly buckled Campemai in. Without the straps, he would be bouncing around the plane like a rag doll. Growing concerned, Paul throttled back, slowing to one hundred miles an hour in an effort to ease the turbulence, and switched on the instrument lights. For a moment he considered turning around to try another way over the storm, but that would use more fuel.

Lightning flashed—a searing, white burst that fried the retinas of their eyes. Fucelli had never heard thunder in the sky, where there is no echo; its hollow explosion, flat, unnatural and hellish, shook him to his bones. For a few seconds, Paul was helplessly blind. As the instruments gradually emerged from the blackness, he turned the cockpit lights to full bright, hoping his eyes would grow accustomed to the light so the next flash would not blind him as long. What was going on here? Only a few moments ago they had been safely on top of the clouds! Two more flashes turned their faces to white, sweat-gleaming specters, and more dead, flat explosions shivered them. "We'll be out of this in a minute," he called back to Fucelli, but his words were lost in the general roar.

At least he hoped they would soon be out of it, for the sheer exertion of keeping *Eighty-six Zulu* under control was drawing beads of sweat from his forehead. He flew like a master, hunched in concentration, his gleaming face like flint in the instrument lights as he wrestled the wheel and rudder pedals. In the frenzied air, most of his instruments oscillated uselessly, so he flew by the gyrocompass, tachometer, and artificial horizon, keeping the horizon bar level and the little bug, which symbolized his plane, in its center. This was no easy task, for with each jolt, the bug jumped mischievously and the horizon bar would fly askew. He opened the throttle to pick up speed. Rough air or not, at one hundred miles an hour the plane's response to the controls was too sluggish, and he needed all the control he could get.

A curious elation gripped him. He was doing what few men could do. Thank goodness they had not retreated before the elements. He was taking the worst the storm could dish out, and he was master of it. Campemai's life would be saved.

Even what happened next did not at first shake his confidence. Without warning, a giant fist struck them from above and a terrific impact shuddered through the plane. The instrument panel blurred for the startled Paul Graham as he was thrown upward against his painfully cutting belt, and he and Fucelli floated against their harnesses as *Eighty-six Zulu* fell from under them like an elevator. They had hit the granddaddy of all downdrafts. The startled instruments came back into focus and confirmed they were going down, down so fast the vertical speed indicator hit the stop at four thousand feet per minute.

Up! We must go up again. Watching the bar of the artificial horizon, Paul leveled the wings, pulled nose up, and opened the throttle to full takeoff power. Yet they continued down, their stomachs floating to their throats, while the propeller clawed helplessly against this falling torrent of air and water.

Paul was not so much frightened as awed by the unbelievable force driving them down toward the jungle. Even though powerless to stop it, he knew they would fly out of the downdraft before it could crash them. And he was proved right. In another shuddering impact the DeVoss seemed to stop in midair as it collided with an updraft like a stone wall. The two men were slammed down against their seats, the blood draining from their heads, as the DeVoss shot skyward again. *Oh Lord, how much can the wings take?* Paul had no more control over the vertical direction of his plane than a falling leaf. The artificial horizon screamed that the plane was standing almost on its tail. He shoved the wheel forward and checked his airspeed indicator. He was appalled to see it lying dead on the peg below fifty miles an hour. Simultaneously the vertical speed indicator and altimeter stopped moving.

He stared, dumbfounded. *Come now, give me sensible readings!* Solid pressure on the seat of his pants told him that they were going up like a shot and that the instruments were obvious liars. *What is wrong? What is wrong?* In its surprising way, his subconscious had the answer, from his many years in the sky. The Pitot tube outside on the wing, source of equalizing air for the instruments, must be clogged with water. This meant that the pressure instruments, the altimeter, vertical speed indicator, and airspeed indicator, were dead, useless.

For the first time since entering the storm, Paul

felt the insidious rise of panic. *This is the way it happens, Graham. Lose a few instruments here, add a little dizziness and confusion there, a little panic. Suddenly in the twisting darkness, you're in big trouble, and you die.*

He fought it, pushing the snake back down into its den, suppressing those nagging thoughts from the depths of his mind. So those instruments were dead. Let them go. He would still control the plane, sense his speed by the pressure of the slipstream against the controls, keep the wings and nose level with the artificial horizon. He began to feel that he could master the storm as, watching the artificial horizon, he leveled out, felt the air pressure rise solid against his controls, watched the tachometer rise to a cruising level. There, he had the speed under reasonable control, and in a few seconds they flew out of the updraft. No, it would not happen to him, Fucelli, and Campemai; they would not die.

Thus for the next few minutes Paul flew through the pounding rain and darkness, oblivious to his throbbing pulse pumping adrenaline through his veins. Fucelli, steeled, fighting nausea, clutched the seat with both hands as though if he let go, he would be flung from the plane. Both men still believed, perhaps unrealistically, that they would make it. Paul dismissed the fact that he could no longer read his airspeed, although the control of airspeed was life itself.

He refused to consider the miles of trackless jungle below, or the fact that he could not tell his height above it. The fuel gauges were nearer empty now than when he had last checked them an eternity ago. But they would reach Colonia, he insisted, because he, Paul Graham, was flying as only men with thousands of hours in the air can fly. And he would continue to do so.

It came as a shock to both men that the impersonal storm would so casually overwhelm them. Lightning flashed again, and as *Eighty-six Zulu* flew that moment into an invisible, vicious air shear, the hollow thunder rolled a fanfare heralding their doom. A bomb seemed to explode under the tail, and at the same time an invisible fist drove the nose down. Startled cries erupted from both men, cries lost as they spun downward through the dark cavern of clouds. The plane gained dangerous speed as it dived, while the controls stiffened in the frenzied slipstream.

Up! Paul's battered senses commanded. *Get the nose up; this plane must slow down! But which way is up? Which way is level? Instruments, tell me which way is level!*

The bar of the artificial horizon lay cockeyed, almost perpendicular in its case. He reacted instinctively to level the wings, yet as he punched the right rudder and twisted in the right aileron, the horizon bar refused to move. For a bewildered second he stared unbelieving, not realizing that the instrument itself was ruined, its gyroscope hopelessly tumbled in the impact of a few seconds before. His last flight instrument was gone.

Paul was unable to level his wings. And because the wings were banked, when he pulled back the wheel, instead of climbing, the plane only pulled itself into a downward spiraling turn. Worse yet, the centrifugal force of this turn, a solid pressure on the seat, made Paul believe he was climbing when he was actually spiraling earthward. This is the illusion of the "graveyard spiral," the most insidious killer since men first flew blind in the clouds.

The first indication that they were not climbing came when Paul realized that his airspeed was staying high—too high. Judging from the stiffness of the controls, it was probably near two hundred miles per hour. He cautiously pulled the wheel back more toward his stomach. *Careful with the wings, kid. Engine rpm's staying high; propeller being fanned by the slipstream. We're still going too fast! More back pressure on the wheel–* G force smashed him into his seat, making his cheeks sag, drawing blood from his brain. But the engine still windmilled fast; their airspeed was still too high. *Oh Lord, how long before the wings fold? Why won't the plane slow down?*

Paul's eyes fell on the still functioning compasses as they revolved slowly, slowly. Was the plane turning in circles? Paul's blood ran cold as he realized he had fallen into that ancient aeronautical trap. "Oh God!" he gasped a prayer. How long had they been spiraling down? How long before trees would burst through the dark, rain-splattered windshield? His heart dissolved in guilt as he realized that with his God-defying pride, he had killed them all. The storm was winning, as any fool might have known it would.

Over the years, some of his friends had died in air crashes, and Paul sometimes wondered what it had been like for them. In the last seconds before death were they panic-stricken? Resigned? Now he was finding out for himself. Nancy flashed into his thoughts so vividly he could see her. "Oh God," he sobbed again. They had failed each other so miserably. "Forgive me," he prayed. "Oh, Lord, forgive me for all this."

How long does it take to repent? It takes only as long as for a man to change his mind about himself, for the Bible promises, "If we confess our sins, he is faithful and just to forgive us our sins, and to cleanse us from all unrighteousness."*Christ, who had waited so patiently for his servant to come back, was there, and Paul knew that the sudden wash of comfort, the sudden clarity of thought was from his Saviour.

No, they were not dead yet. To recover from

---
*1 John 1:9

the spiral, Paul knew he must somehow level the wings. But there were no instruments left to portray the axis of his wings—except the compasses. Maybe he could use them. If he could stop the compasses' slow turning, he would know that the plane was in a straight dive. And if it was in a straight dive, with a neutral rudder, the wings must be level.

Even as he followed this logical sequence, his reflexes responded. Compasses revolving to the left meant the plane was spiraling to the right. He punched left rudder, twisted left aileron, and felt the horrible, crushing pressure ease as the plane rolled out of the turn. They must now be in a straight dive. Very cautiously he pulled back the wheel again, fighting the impulse to jerk it back before they smashed into the ground, for a quick, backward move of the wheel now could very well tear off their wings. Slowly he eased it back, and again the pressure of G force crushed them downward. But this time—*Oh, thank You, Lord*—the tachometer began to drop, and the horrible stiffness of the controls began to ease. Paul knew they were leveling off, slowing down. *How magnificent to escape from a graveyard spiral with only a gyrocompass and tachometer!* Paul knew that his own thoughts and reflexes had not saved them. The Lord had answered his abject prayer. The Lord had directed him as surely as if His own loving hands had taken the controls.

OK, watch it. Don't pull up for so long you lose all your speed and stall. Don't forget the engine; give it some gas! Paul flew on, concentrating, through the rain. The fact that they had missed death by twenty seconds seemed quite irrelevant.

Suddenly both men were aware of the engine noise again. There was no rain, but they were still blind in the clouds, sailing on air wonderfully smooth. Paul was too preoccupied to cheer, but Fucelli looked up from his nauseated misery as shocked with the relative quiet as he had been with the rain and lightning. A few minutes ago he had fully expected to die, picturing Marilyn and Laurie as they withdrew from the mission compound in tears without him. Now the ridiculous thought flashed through his mind that perhaps they were really dead after all, simply flying through the heavenly mist.

But a few seconds later, the mist flashed away as if they had burst through a paper curtain, and both men stared at blue sky darkening in the twilight. They were too numb to cheer; but slowly it registered that they had come through the storm alive. Above them arched the deepening purple vault of sky. Below, the jungle trees grew dim in a vaporous evening mist. They flew among scattered puffs of clouds that seemed like calves straggling behind the main herd. And behind them was the chastening storm that had driven Paul Graham back to his Saviour.

As a tribute to Paul's navigation, only fifteen miles ahead, Viejo Montana rose from the mist like the dark hump back of a primeval monster. They were not far off course, for Colonia lay only a mile from the mountain's base.

His nausea fading, Fucelli unbuckled from the jump seat and examined Campemai to see if the turbulence had caused any additional bleeding. It had not, and he thrust his pale face up between the two front seats and tapped Paul's shoulder. "Thanks, Paul," he smiled. "I think Campemai came through the wringer OK too."

Paul's face was blank with a tired peace. "Thank the Lord," he told Fucelli. "He's the One who carried us through that thing."

Fucelli was surprised to hear that from Paul Graham. But maybe in the storm something had occurred. "Wow!" He said. "I've never been through a pounding like that in my life! I don't see how you did it, Paul. I really don't."

But the pilot was not smiling, for some reason, and Fucelli, following his gaze downward, suddenly guessed why. "What about that fog, Paul?"

"You know, I should've suspected it. Warm air behind a warm front, you get ground fog." A sardonic grin flickered and vanished on Paul's haggard face. "Our problems aren't over yet, Fudd. We can use the mountain there as a reference, and we can find Colonia with no trouble. But whether we can see the runway, or anything else, I don't know yet. Like I say, we might have problems."

Fucelli's jaw fell. *This is unbelievable. It isn't fair!* "You mean we can't land after all this?"

Paul waved toward the fuel gauges, both pointers resting on empty. "We'll land, all right. We'll definitely land very soon—when the engine quits."

Fucelli fell silent, knowing that their chances of a successful blind landing in fog were zero. Slumping into the jump seat, he poured out his heart to God. Paul watched the timbered ridge of Viejo Montana drift closer. Soon, beyond the mountain he could see only more mist hugging the ground like a milky liquid. "As You will, Father," he breathed. "I don't understand—" No, he did not understand why the Lord would bring them through the storm and then leave a mist over the earth. But he knew he would never again question the Lord's doing. "I accept Your will, Father."

Maybe they had presumed too much on God's mercy, after all. For men simply cannot expect to challenge such storms and survive unscathed.

8

Home Before Dark

In the stifling headquarters of Interior Evangelism, Savillas opened both windows of the radio room; in crept sodden, dripping heat, and the pages of the radio log were as limp as the five anxious Christians gathered there. Puente, at the table beside Savillas beneath the huge Chaco map, tried not to appear absurd as he tied red marker flares to his hunting arrows. "When Paulo's motor comes," he said defensively, "we will light flares along the runway, and I will shoot these into the air." He eyed Savillas guardedly. "Paulo would be blind if he failed to see them."

"I told you before," Savillas snapped, "it's a wise thing. I just do not expect to see Graham here tonight, that's all."

Seated by Savillas, Nancy sighed, eyeing the dial of the shortwave as it glowed in mocking silence, refusing to divulge the whereabouts of her husband and his passengers. "Who else can we call?" she pleaded.

Savillas shook his head. They had called Bahia Negra, Puerto Sastre, Coronel Varisca, Filadelfia and several ranches in between. But there had been no trace of *Eighty-six Zulu* since Paul Graham left Asoe some ninety minutes ago. "I maintain," Savillas soothed, "he's landed in a field or on a road somewhere to wait out the storm. We will see him tomorrow morning." He smiled broadly, reassuring. "Do not become worried so soon, Nancy. He is safe somewhere, and you will soon have your farm together."

The remark stung; Nancy at that moment was not at all worried about a farm. "And you don't think he would fly through the storm, even though Campemai may die tonight?"

"The Indian would die for sure if their plane crashed, wouldn't he? How foolish that would be. My opinion is, to fly through such a storm would be very poor judgment. I am sure Paulo didn't do it."

"If he used good judgment." Her voice grew strained. "But this would be his last flight before we left for home. And I know he would never be content to go home knowing he'd let somebody die. I know him too well, and that makes me more guilty." At the window she leaned wearily on the sill. "If we had bought a radio instead of our passage home—he could've refueled at Bahia and flown somewhere else with Campemai, couldn't he?"

Savillas smiled sadly. "Nancy, it is quite useless to think of past things, things already done."

"Unless you can make up for them in the future—if there's a chance in the future." On impulse she turned to Dr. Pearson, who, in a corner chair, was seemingly dozing but in reality was praying very hard. "Will you and Margaret talk with me in your office?" she asked.

In Pearson's cluttered office they talked, as they had done on a night months ago. Nancy buried her face in her hands momentarily as white-haired Margaret Pearson put a comforting arm around her. "I won't cry," she quavered, "because there's too much to be said now. But it looks like judgment day for me, doesn't it?"

"That is very premature," said Pearson, even as a tight voice betrayed his doubt.

"No, it isn't." She did not tell them of the strange words intercepted on her radio, "He loved you till he died." But there were enough other obvious reasons. "Even if he got through the storm, he couldn't land anywhere in a fog like this."

"We don't believe he tried to penetrate the storm." Pearson said. "But—"

"I believe he did." There followed an awkward silence before she took a deep breath and continued. "What I want to tell both of you is, last night—last night I began coming back to the Lord." She smiled at Pearson. "That sermon from Puente started it, I guess. And then with

Ijomejene last night—I think the Lord arranged that—it was like things used to be back in the beginning. I had a taste of being in fellowship with Christ again, you know?"

They knew. Nancy, a Christian, spoke of things only other Christians can understand: fellowship with the Lord Jesus, and knowing His will—concepts unknown to one who has never been redeemed.

"Just before I came up here," she went on, "I was debating with myself whether I wanted to give my life back to the Lord again. Can you imagine debating something like that? Oh, I didn't say it in just that way; I was thinking of all the reasons I could never serve Him again, you know? But it all boils down to our faith and our will, doesn't it?"

"Yes, it does," smiled Margaret.

"And just now," Nancy said, "when I was talking to Alfredo about how, if Paul had bought the radio, he would be safe now, I finally saw what an ugly thing my attitude has been. It's ruined my witness for the Lord, it's harmed the mission here, and it's killed Paul." Her voice dissolved in tears.

"We don't know that, child!" Margaret Pearson soothed.

"I know it. I don't know how, but I do." After a few moments sobbing she regained control. "But right now, please pray with me, will you? Pray that no matter what happens to Paul, I'll accept it as God's will. I want to love the Lord. I've already hurt too many people."

Thank You, Lord, Pearson prayed silently. *Is this what it took to bring Nancy back? Obviously so. For how well You know each of Your children.* He prayed with Nancy, "Oh, Lord Jesus, Thou who calmed the sea with only a word, Thou who art master of storm and rain, and fog, we commit to Thy perfect loving will Thy children Paul and Nancy. Father, we pray for the safety of Paul, Ed, and Campemai. Please hold them in Your almighty arms. Join us all again in safety that we may serve Thee together once again. And for Nancy, we pray that—"

From the sky an engine murmured, faint and far to the northwest. Pearson stopped praying, and they stared in silence, each wondering if the others heard it too. Then they burst from the office into the radio room. Puente had already left to set his flares, and Savillas was shouting into the microphone.

"Paulo, we can hear you. You're northwest of us. Paulo, if you can hear me, rev your prop up and back as a signal. Over."

They waited for the telltale whining rise and fall of his engine. But Nancy's smile soon faded as the faraway motor remained steady. Paul's radio was still dead. "But it's heading this way! Can he see—how can he see us?"

"He cannot see us," Savillas said crisply. "He

is guessing by the mountain, I'm sure." He pounded the desk furiously. "His radio is a faithless wretch! I could direct him to the field. Of a truth I could!" Stalking to the door he called back, "Nancy, keep calling him, for his radio may yet blip on. I will help Puente."

Nancy sat trembling in front of the radio. In the engine's sound Paul spoke to her from the sky—near, but so far away.

Outside, Puente and Savillas dashed with their flares through the steaming mist. "Now you may test your *extrano aviso*," Savillas puffed.

"And tonight you will see Paulo and I laugh as we thank God together."

Savillas, at one end of the clay airstrip, ripped the tape on a flare, and the plastic striking cap flew off and rolled away. After a few seconds' frantic search, he found it and scratched the phosphorus head. "Light, will you!" Finally it flared into brilliant red; he dropped it and ran down the strip to drop another. *Faster, Alfredo*, he puffed to himself. *Before the plane passes over, Lord, we need a hole in this fog. No, we need a corridor!*

At that moment Paul was soaring above the darkened summit of Viejo Montana. Eastward in the arching, purple sky, the first stars were faintly visible, amassing to attack sunset's last glow above the western storm clouds; then stars would rule the sky. Time and fuel were running out for Paul; he could not find Colonia. The town was only a mile from the mountain's base, and he could not find it! Paul was all the more frustrated because the blanket of ground mist one thousand feet below was really quite thin, and when looking straight down, he could distinguish hazy, darkened features on the surface. But looking ahead, at the oblique angle necessary to find his way, nothing was visible behind that white curtain lying so gently on the earth.

His stomach contracted hopelessly as they flew on, moment after moment, a lost bird over the sea. Still, in the small circle of visibility moving beneath them like a shadow, he saw only the hazy outlines of Quebracho forest. How could he miss anything as big as Colonia? He had flown approaches over this area a hundred times, yet what little he could see below was all utterly strange.

After a few moments it appeared not only possible but probable that they would never find Colonia, that they would play a hopeless game of hide-and-seek until their fuel was gone. And then, Paul knew, when they descended into the ground fog, he would have to land completely blind—a sure crash. "So be it, Lord," he breathed. "But I pray by Your grace we'll survive."

It was then, when he was approaching possible death, that Paul knew the wonder of his salvation. He knew that if in a few minutes he should stand before God, he would do so with his sins covered by the blood of Jesus. *Thank You, Lord. What horror it would be,* he thought, *to face death without that assurance.* He thought of Campemai. Had the Indian ever accepted Christ, or was his soul hanging now on the brink of hell? *Father, especially let him live,* Paul prayed again. No man should die without knowing this wonderful One, Jesus Christ.

By now it was obvious that they had missed Colonia. Paul turned back toward the mountain, this time making a pass further north, hoping still to see the village lights below. And while there was time, he gave instructions to Fucelli; there were blankets and padding in the baggage nook aft of the cargo area. He should strap this padding around Campemai. "And turn the stretcher so his feet are against the front bulkhead. You can still fasten the aft end of the stretcher; and it will be better if he takes the impact feet first."

Impact? The chilling word shattered what was left of Fucelli's joy at surviving the storm.

"And when you finish with Campemai," Paul went on, "wrap some of the padding around yourself and buckle in the jump seat tight, OK? And Fudd, look, just before we go in, hold a pad over your face. That's for Marilyn."

Fucelli nodded solemnly, hoping Paul could not detect the boiling misery of his stomach. "Come on, Paul, we'll still make it—won't we?"

Paul pointed down. "When we go down into

that, I can't guarantee what we'll hit. Better buckle up back there like I said. You and Campemai should be all right."

"And you?"

"Well, sure. Me too." Paul paused a minute. "But look, Fudd, if anything does happen to me, tell Nancy that things were all right between me and the Lord, will you? The Lord knocked me off my high horse back in the storm there, and we're back together now."

Fucelli thought of the hymn "Nothing Between my Soul and the Saviour." "Welcome back, brother," he growled. He punched Paul's shoulder. "But you tell Nancy that yourself."

Fucelli eased back past the porthole window, dreading to hear Campemai's groans when he moved the stretcher. Something far below caught his eye. Joyfully he clambered back up front. "Did you see that, Paul? Over there. Over there! Like a red Roman-candle shooting up!"

Whatever it was had disappeared again in the fog, but Paul immediately swung his plane in the direction of Fucelli's pointing finger. "Couldn't be a flare!" he shouted, not knowing Puente had just shot aloft his last marker flare with his prized fiberglass bow.

As both men peered downward, Colonia suddenly emerged directly below them. They could see the miniature tile roofs with window lights muted in the fog like fireflies in a forest. Without realizing, Fucelli was pounding Paul's shoulder. "That's it!"

"Don't take your eyes off it!" Paul snapped. He fought the urge to throw his plane into a turn before the lights below should be lost again. He held it straight, looking, hoping.

In a few seconds, what he had hoped to see emerged through the mist: tiny pinpoints of red, far below, where Savillas and Puente had marked the airstrip. He banked into the steep, circling turn. "We've got the strip!" he croaked.

Fucelli peered below and saw the row of flares only several feet long. *Graham! How will we land on that?* Only then did he suddenly realize how completely the fog was confusing his perception.

"Hurry up! Hurry and fix Campemai," Paul shouted. "We'll try to get down before our gas runs out."

With hope and despair tangled together in his stomach, Fucelli began the difficult task of moving the stretcher in a banked, circling airplane. At the same time he was fighting a dreadful nausea.

While he worked, Paul held the turn and, with the Jeppesen, tried to plot an approach to the ground. Somehow he must fly a series of turns, a pattern that would bring him to the ground at the airfield now directly below. And he must do it with no flight instruments at all, except a compass. OK, no instruments. But he knew from long experience that, with the engine throttled back to eighteen hundred revolutions per minute and with the nose lowered to maintain a speed of ninety miles an hour, the DeVoss would lose altitude at a rate of five hundred feet per minute. On this basis he would plan the approach, knowing that his success would hinge on his ability to sense the plane's speed and angle of descent, as an experienced rider feels out his horse. While his plane hung, tiny in the paling sky, his adrenaline-keyed mind worked through the approach. They were, he estimated, one thousand feet above the ground. He would roll out of his turn at right angles to the row of flares, establish a descent rate, and hold a heading of 260 degrees for twenty seconds. Then he would have to turn onto a downwind leg of 350 degrees which, held for forty seconds, would establish the length of their final approach. Then a base leg of eighty degrees held for twenty seconds would bring them back in line with the airstrip. From this position, he would fly a final approach of 170 degrees and at the end of forty seconds, hope to see the flare-lighted runway.

Of course, it was preposterous to think they would actually hit the target. Perhaps they would hit the boulder-strewn clearing just ahead of the runway. He would settle for that. Or maybe Puente's cornfield and garden. But if he saw only trees or, worse yet, the rooftops of Colonia, he must open the throttle and zoom upward to try again.

Fucelli finished strapping himself in then, nauseated and feeling guilty that he was so protected while Paul, up front, was so exposed. Then Paul, with his heart pounding, began the approach. He throttled back till the engine rumble softened to eighteen hundred revolutions per minute, lowered the nose, and felt his plane begin settling from under him. His every nerve strained to sense the speed of *Eighty-six Zulu*, to estimate how fast they were sliding out of the sky. "Oh Lord, guide my hands as You did in the storm," he breathed. By his wristwatch, compass, and tachometer—and instinct—he flew his planned pattern while the mist, now darkened to a lusterless gray, rose slowly to meet him. The occasional glances he stole straight below revealed only strange field or forest. But of course he could not expect anything to look familiar in the murky half-light. Soon it would be over, one way or another. He felt a brief exhilaration at the thought that they might soon be down and safe in spite of the storm, in spite of the fog. But more likely he, at least, would soon be dead. He thought of the verse, "Whether we live therefore, or die, we are the Lord's."[*] *But Lord, if we die, what will happen to the Edigo? Or to the mission? And what will Nancy do—* He shut her from his mind; he couldn't afford nerves of jelly now.

---

[*]Romans 14:8

The seconds passed relentlessly, and now it was time to begin the final approach. He swung right onto 170 degrees, appalled that he could still see nothing ahead except the sea of featureless, gray mist rising to meet him. *Oh Father, help me.* It was crazy to descend blind into that! Both fuel gauges were past empty. *Don't quit now. Let the engine run a little longer, just a little longer.* Straight below were only ghostly treetops, now uncomfortably close. Thirty seconds to go. He lowered full flaps to slow *Eighty-six Zulu* and lowered the nose a fraction, trying to keep their descent rate steady. *Careful with the speed, kid.* As they dropped closer to the fog it flowed beneath them, giving the dangerous illusion they were speeding faster and faster. Paul resisted it, knowing that to slow down too much now would invite the stall and spin which would kill them all. *Oh, for an airspeed indicator!*

The fog began to envelope him like the gray arms of death. His eyes strained to penetrate the curtain; his nerves were poised for instant action. Straight below, underbrush was passing by. At least they were out of the forest. He continued holding 170 degrees, held their descent rate steady. Soon he should see the ground ahead.

Suddenly, off to the left, there appeared the red glow of flares. He had no time to cry for joy. Even more miraculous, the runway emerged clearly, only three hundred yards ahead, as he descended through a layer of fog. In a flash, though, it was gone. It appeared again through another hole. The sudden flashes of visibility bewildered Paul. The plane seemed to stop and then leap forward while the earth teetered spasmodically. He was growing disoriented! *Oh, Lord, no.* Instinctively he sought the instrument panel, but there were no functioning flight instruments left. Now he had lost all sense of speed. Unnerved, he opened the throttle to climb, while sweat flowed down his face in rivulets.

There is a pitiless law of the universe that our mistakes carry in themselves their own penalty. As he opened the throttle, the fuel-starved engine backfired several times and died; *Eighty-six Zulu* staggered downward. This was it.

Fucelli's stomach erupted, and he looked away to avoid spewing the filth on Campemai. Then he remembered to hold the pad against his face. A shocked and numb Paul barely had time to cut the master switch to prevent fire as he glared into the opaque mist. Treetops were looming in the windshield. These were the trees that bordered the south end of the airfield he had just missed. The snare had closed, the snare of circumstance, the snare of time and weather and faulty judgment, the snare of the faithless acts of he and Nancy, the snare that had shadowed him for months. *Now there is nothing on earth that will buy another foot of altitude, another knot of airspeed.*

On reflex, he pulled back the wheel. But *Eighty-six Zulu* simply did not have enough speed left; in her wings there was no life, and she refused to climb. They brushed over in a shower of leaves and broken branches and then plummeted earthward. Paul felt no fear, only betrayal that his plane would no longer obey the commands from his racing brain. He was lifting, and the world caved in on him as *Eighty-six Zulu* impacted like thunder, nose first and to the left, wrenching off the left wing and buckling the fuselage. The wreck continued, sliding through underbrush, bucking over rocks before finally halting, swathed in a cloud of oil smoke. And the cloud reluctantly drifted away like a departing soul from the carcass of *Eighty-six Zulu*.

9

As the Stars Forever

Moments before the crash, a small crowd had formed at Interior Evangelism's hangar. Compassionate, capable Mennonites and some members of the volunteer fire brigade alerted by Paul Graham's engine overhead, gathered in the hot, foggy evening. And horses tethered in front of the house, stamping restlessly, seemed to sense the group's apprehension.

At the clinic, Dr. Brubacher and his nurse were scrubbing down for the operation he must soon perform if Paul was fortunate enough to land without mishap. Otherwise there would be three patients instead of one—or perhaps only funerals.

Knowing she had planned to leave in two days, Nancy's neighbors at the airfield watched her with trepidation. As she stood beside Margaret Pearson, straight, with hands cupped over her nose and mouth and her eyes closed in silent prayer, they gathered protectively around her and fervently hoped no further misfortune would come to one who had so recently buried her son. But their hopes died as the plane soared over like a huge, dark bat; and there were involuntary cries as from far out in the field rolled the hollow crash, exploding like a shock wave through the fog, and the shriek of tearing metal that seemed to go on forever.

Several mounted riders were already galloping toward the place from which the sound had come. "In the jeep!" Savillas barked as he, Puente, and a huge fireman, Gert Unruh, piled in with a fire extinguisher and first-aid cases. Nancy jumped in the back.

"Best stay here!" Savillas snapped as he started the engine. But she didn't move, and, catlike, he leapt out to grasp her roughly by the shoulder. "I demand you stay here!" he snarled.

Her wet, resolute eyes told him she would come, one way or another. *OK. Let her come.* They were wasting time. He only wanted to save her from nightmares the rest of her life.

A groggy Fucelli hung against his harness in the upended fuselage, quite surprised to find himself still alive. Campemai, barely visible in the darkness, was in a heap against the back of the pilot's seat, his hysterical cries like the strangled barking of a dog. He must help the Indian, Fucelli decided; although at the moment he was not sure why. Yes, as long as he was not dead he may as well help Campemai. Acrid smoke stung his nostrils, but the fact that the smoke was filling the plane meant little to him. Clumsily he fumbled for the buckle and, when it released, fell forward against the cargo door. How odd that the door was where the floor should be! He lay there for a moment, coughing and confused, until the sound of shouting approached. There was a great deal of banging around his head and the squeal of tearing metal as the door was wrenched open, and he fell out into the arms of the yellow-bearded Unruh.

Rescuers surged about the plane as Savillas, horrified by orange flames flickering from beneath the crumpled engine compartment, blasted it thoroughly with the extinguisher. *Thank You, Lord, that there was no gasoline left in the ruptured wing; or the plane would've exploded like a bomb.*

Nancy hesitantly approached the shattered plexiglass, what was left of the windshield, and peered through to see Paul in the dim light, surrounded by crumpled aluminum, his white teeth showing through a mask of oil and blood. Whimpering and unable to find the door handle, she began to tear at the metal with her hands, and Savillas gently pulled her away. "Sit down for a moment. Don't look at him. We'll get him out. Sit down, please, Nancy."

Campemai was easily extracted through the cargo door; and he and Fucelli were carried off on stretchers, with Fucelli babbling a mixture of Guarani and English to his rescuers. Then, while

Savillas grimly held a flashlight through the broken windshield, Unruh entered through the cargo door to examine the unconscious pilot. A weak, rapid pulse told him Paul was, surprisingly, still alive. Unruh shuddered at the thought of cutting him free while at the same time keeping him alive in spite of blood loss and shock. Now it was sure that even the Indian had a better chance of survival than Paul Graham.

They commented, later, on how Nancy had regained a remarkable calm. How, although sometimes sobbing convulsively like a little child, she had held a cloth against Paul's forehead to stop the bleeding there, and how as he was being cut free, she had held pressure points to slow the bleeding in his legs.

She remembered it mostly in certain vivid scenes like a half-remembered dream—the garish, flickering light of the acetylene torch casting spastic shadows as Unruh cut through the aluminum; and Savillas standing by, a guarding soldier, with the fire extinguisher. There was the deathly pallor of Paul's features in the light, and the Bible verse that rose unaccountably in her mind, "And they that be wise shall shine as the brightness of the firmament; and they that turn many to righteousness as the stars forever and ever."[*] It had come from the Lord, she knew. Was it an epitaph for Paul? Or

---

[*]Daniel 12:3

could it be a promise for their future together? *Which is it, Lord?* she prayed. *If he lives, I promise it will be our future.*

Don't let him die. She had prayed these same words several months ago with her already dead child in her arms. But now there was no ultimatum to the Lord. Gone was the self-righteous anger of past months. That attitude was impossible now, for she knew the crash had come from the rebellion of her and Paul against their Lord. That knowledge was driven home with each wrenching squeal of the crowbar, as the men muttered and sweated to free Paul before he died.

Brubacher was breathing hard, the heavy paunch of his belly rising and falling, and he thought to himself that he was getting too old for this sort of thing. Campemai's surgery had drained him. He had treated many chest wounds of this type, especially during the Chaco war with Bolivia. Of course, he had been much younger then, and the wounds had come from bullets, not barbed spear-points that left the doctor sweating and marveling at the fiendish devices humans conceive to kill their fellows. It had almost killed this Indian, that was certain. But now the lance was out and he had sewn in a tube to drain the fluid. If they could control infection, the Indian would probably survive. That leathery little missionary, Fucelli, would do well also; he had suffered only deep bruises where the harness had cut across him. He would be terribly sore for a time, but, all considered, he was a fortunate man.

It was the pilot, Paul Graham, about whom the doctor was most worried. His left leg was broken in many places, his ankle was a mess of torn nerves and ligaments, he had second-degree burns on the right leg, and a probable concussion. It was beyond the clinic's capabilities; he was not a miracle worker! X-rays must be made. They must transport Paul to Asunción as soon as possible. The sooner the better. Brubacher would do what he could; he would try to keep him alive and hope a night like this would never come again.

Early the next morning, with Nancy and a heavily sedated Paul aboard, Savillas's Helio Courier blasted off the runway into a gloriously clear morning and headed for Asunción. Savillas must pick up a party of sportsmen in the capital and would be gone for several weeks afterward. "But I will pray for Paulo every moment I can," he assured Nancy.

As they passed over Estancia Carambola, Paul began to murmur incoherently and tried to move, his drugged mind stirring to life at the engine's sound. Nancy stroked his face and kissed him. "You're all right, Paul," she said softly. "I'm right here."

"Couldn't find the up button," he muttered.

It was an old joke. Nancy leaned across the seat to tell Savillas, who grinned widely. "That is a good sign. He should do well."

Paul indeed did well. At the Southern Baptist Hospital in Asunción, where Puente had found his Lord, patients were soon commenting on the bright courage of the auburn-haired girl whose husband was the injured pilot. "They're missionaries, you know; the pilot crashed in saving an Edigo Indian. Did you read of it in the *Noticias*?"

"Ah, then that is the reason."

Yes, that must be the reason for a certain buoyance in the face of tragedy. They were missionaries, who, unlike normal people, possessed some sort of mystical nature. In her witnessing, however, Nancy made it clear her strength was in the Saviour she possessed.

On the second day after the crash, Paul opened his eyes to become fully conscious. Having had surgery upon their arrival at the hospital, he was aware of things around him for the first time since the crash. He recognized Nancy and smiled.

"I love you, Paul," she whispered, as her soft hair and tears caressed his face. "I've been wanting to tell you that so badly, and you couldn't hear me!"

"I love you, too, Baby-girl," he murmured. It was a pet name he had not used in several months.

Later that evening, when he was more alert, they talked. "I must have really pranged it." He hesitated, afraid to ask just how badly.

She did not want him to know how ghastly he looked, with patches of beard growing through bruised, oil-seared skin. "You should see the plane," she smiled airily, "it looks a lot worse than you do."

"What about—?"

"They're both great. Campemai is recovering back in Colonia, and Ed didn't even get cut. Yeah! Nothing but bruises."

"Thank God," he sighed with eyes closed. "What a foolish thing, but thank God! Learned—learned some lessons."

Lessons. Sometimes they are learned too late, with only remorse following. Not so for Paul and Nancy. Certainly they knew remorse for the wrecked plane and injuries to Paul and Fucelli. But they knew also the blessings that soon flowed from their tragedy—their renewed love for the Lord and for each other and their decision to stay, if possible, with the mission. That eternal promise to "shine as the stars forever" far outweighed any farm in Virginia. They had prevented a civil war in the Edigo tribe.

Another blessing came when a Christian contractor in Louisiana noticed the news story (a paragraph buried on page 5) about Paul Graham and, instead of trading his used Helio Courier, donated it to Interior Evangelism. Thus Paul's dream plane, which could take off or land in 350 feet, was now the mission's.

Three weeks after the crash, a high-spirited Fucelli and Dr. Pearson brought his heady piece of news. Of course, Paul tried to be enthusiastic, but it was a ruse hard to sustain, for he guessed why the men had come. Yes, the mission would soon have a new airplane. Thank God. But would Paul Graham ever be allowed to fly it?

They talked awhile, of Paul's and Ed's conditions. Then Pearson cleared his throat, his way of announcing, "Gentlemen, it's time for business." Typically, he started on an optimistic note. "Paul, I praise the Lord for your and Nancy's decision to remain with the mission. For me that is a direct answer to prayer; I only regret the answer had to come in this way."

"You and me both," Paul grinned painfully.

"And of course I accept your decision, Paul. But I'm afraid there are going to be some problems involved. The trustees of our mission board in Richmond are pressing me for details on this crash. And, to be brutally candid, they want a recommendation as to whether you should continue as our pilot—assuming, of course, your physical condition permits it."

Nancy squeezed Paul's hand reassuringly as Pearson went on. "It seems organizations like MAF and JAARS can fly worldwide, facing even more hazardous conditions than ours, and yet go for years without mishap."

Paul finished the line of reasoning for him. "And the board wants to know, with a little, one-plane operation over mostly flat land, how I managed to wipe out the airplane?"

"To be blunt, yes. And I don't know what to tell them, Paul. I must be completely honest with the board and still be fair to everyone involved down here. Some heads may roll over this, including my own." Pearson stopped, unsure how to continue.

"That's going to be a tough report," Paul smiled weakly. "But believe me, I've had plenty of time, lying here, to think this whole thing through, Travis. I think we should start with a basic premise. Now, accident reports seem to bear this out: a crash never has only one cause."

Amid the faint smell of alcohol and disinfectant, Paul discussed that phenomenon so long known to crash and safety investigators—the subtle interplay of physchological stress with flight circumstances and even the aircraft design itself. "Usually there are causes going back for months, and the way in which these factors will converge at a critical time is astounding. Usually the pilot is only one link in this tragic chain," Paul said, "but the pilot is the one person ultimately responsible for his aircraft."

"Would you say then, Paul, that your mental condition was one of those causes?"

The pilot grimaced. "I'm afraid so. My spiritual condition, too, but even more so."

"Well, here is why I asked that." Pearson leaned forward intensely. "The night you crashed, Savillas was of the opinion that to fly through such a storm would be suicidal. He didn't think you would do it, for it would be extremely poor judgment for whatever reason. Now, do you agree with that?"

Ah, Travis, your questions are so simple and penetrating. Paul nodded slowly. "I have to agree with that, Travis. It was suicidal. I knew it even then."

So the indictment was delivered by Paul himself. They were all embarrassed and silent for a moment while Pearson stared at the floor.

Fucelli was first to break the silence. "I put a lot of pressure on Paul," he muttered. "And part of the blame for this will have to fall on me. But, Travis, for the life of me, were we so wrong? Maybe we both forgot who our Lord is; we took matters into our own hands. And I'm not proud of that. But what if we hadn't gone through the storm? I'm not so sure I wouldn't do it again."

He glanced apologetically at Paul, who muttered back, "Forget it. I was the pilot."

"Thank God you were, brother. Not many men could have got us through that."

"But there is a contradiction here, Paul." Pearson looked up suddenly. "This mental condition, this phobia that overcame you during the months since Eddy was killed, it produced fear didn't it? So how could this prompt an act of courage, even though the act was irrational?"

"That's just it, Travis. It was fear. I was terrified of going home knowing that I'd failed, that I'd let Campemai die because of my cowardice. Do you see? I was more afraid of failure than of—of dying." Paul's voice grew strained. "And once I decided I didn't care if I died, it was like a strange calm came over me. But I learned later, neither that decision nor that calm was from the Lord."

"How do you know?"

"I'd rather not say." Paul reddened. "It was something that happened in the storm."

"I think you'd best tell me, Paul! We've some hard decisions to make here; let's level with each other."

Paul reluctantly told them of how he had flown so well through the storm, cocksure in his own flying ability, until the "graveyard spiral" trapped him. "I knew then we were as good as dead." Paul breathed deeply and looked at the ceiling. "And, Travis, in a flash I saw it all clearly—what had been happening to me over the past months. I thought I could get through the storm on my own—found out I couldn't. And I repented in a split second." Paul smiled. "The Lord keeps His word, doesn't He? He guided me out of that spiral in a way I could never have done myself. He saved our lives. And He's been with me ever since, even during the crash." He grinned sheepishly at Nancy.

"You weren't going to tell me about that spiral, were you?" she smiled.

"Didn't want you to know how close we came."

"You can tell me those things now," she scolded gently. Paul breathed deeply again and smiled. What a wife he had!

"So you saw it all clearly," Pearson said. "You're blessed. Most people go through life without ever once seeing clearly with the eyes of their soul. But obviously you do. And Fucelli tells me you were indeed a different man when you came out of the storm. Would you say, Paul, that you've been cured?"

Paul looked into Pearson's dim, direct eyes. "I'm sure of it."

"That being so, then, I want an honest answer to this question. If the same circumstances occurred today, what would you do?"

A fly buzzing loudly in the silence flicked past them before Paul answered. "I would land at Paso Moro. I wouldn't try to go through that front."

"Even if Campemai were sure to die?"

Paul bit his lip. "Yes, even if he would die. It simply isn't rational to risk an airplane and three lives to save one. I wouldn't do it."

Pearson smiled his approval. "And yet, Dr. Brubacher tells me, with the lance imbedded as it was, Campemai couldn't have lived more than a few hours. Had you landed at Paso Moro, Paul, Campemai would be dead today, and how many more Edigo would've died in the ensuing war? But thank the Lord, he's alive."

"Yes," growled Fucelli. "And as of now there have been no revenge killings at all. Inacarai and Campemai talked on the shortwave with each other yesterday. Yeah," Fucelli laughed, "you should've seen him! Marilyn says Inacarai is very impressed with his son's recovery. And I think, Paul, there will be many Edigo souls in heaven because you saved Campemai's life."

Pearson removed his glasses and stared blankly out the window at Asunción for several minutes. "Very well," he said finally. "There is only one way this whole affair makes any sense at all. Paul, is it possible that Satan was weaving a snare to kill you, Ed, and Campemai? Listen. First there was this darkness of mind which overcame you and Nancy. We know this was spawned by Satan, certainly. Then the leaking propeller that forced your stop at Varisca outpost and prevented your taking on gasoline. And, of course, Campemai's being stabbed was surely Satan's doing, perhaps working through Paje-de. And then your radio, Paul." Pearson smiled softly. "It was sin, of course, when you spent that money for passage home, rather than purchasing the new unit; consequently, Satan had authority to use that radio against you. And then the storm front—they tell me it was the most violent in years. The Bible indicates Satan can partially control the weather at times. All considered, it was an elaborate snare indeed."

"It's possible," Fucelli murmured.

"And then," Pearson went on with growing excitement, "see how the Lord defeated Satan's plan at the last minute! Paul, did the Lord permit your psychological instability because He knew that in your normal frame of mind, you would never challenge such a storm? And then Campemai would've died, wouldn't he? But God turned the snare around and used it to save Campemai. It also kept you and Nancy here with the mission, and it gave us a new and safer airplane. What a master stroke that was!"

And the group sat for a moment contemplating if this indeed had been a particularly vicious skirmish in the conflict of the ages, though on this side of eternity they would never know for sure. But Nancy could not help thinking of the verses quoted on that night several months ago, "O the depth of the riches both of the wisdom and knowledge of God! how unsearchable are his judgments and his ways past finding out! For who has known the mind of the Lord, or who became his counselor?"[†]

Several months later, the board, on Pearson's

[†]Romans 11:33

recommendation, approved Paul Graham to continue as pilot for the Chaco region of Interior Evangelism. But Paul was seven months in recovering. He and Nancy returned to the United States, where, at Bethesda, Maryland, Paul's shattered ankle was operated on a second and third time. Even with the pain and, worse for Paul, the forced inactivity, those months were blessed. The couple visited all their supporting churches, renewing acquaintance with the pastors and local Christians who kept the Grahams close to their hearts in prayer and financial support.

During this time, Nancy and Paul spent two months at the Sheffield farm, and several times they drove, in the Blazer, to the top of the wooded knoll which could be theirs if they would only say the word. *To have a house here among the trees and rolling blue mountains—* Nancy considered it. And for a brief moment, she pictured Eddy as he would have looked, a farm boy running through the July sunshine. *No, no.* She had something far more precious than a farm and house, something few people in this world have. She had Jesus Christ; better yet, she knew His will and knew she was in it. To be in the perfect, loving will of Christ was joy and peace, and all else the world could offer was surely a drab second best. And to make it perfect, she had the love of a man who knew this same Lord and same will. That conviction never left her for long; when it did, there was the limp Paul carried for years afterward to remind her of the consequences of self will.

They returned to Paraguay in October. Spring again: a time to renew. Paul eyed the Helio Courier like a boy on Christmas morning, and as soon as he could break away from the tasks of moving in, he and Savillas began the series of check rides. Limping out to examine his new plane, Paul noticed a small tab on the bright orange rudder. This Helio had rudder-trim control, which would greatly ease the strain of the rudder pedals on his tender ankle. "Lord," he prayed softly, aloud, "You think of everything, don't You?"

Moody Press, a ministry of the Moody Bible Institute, is designed for education, evangelization, and edification. If we may assist you in knowing more about Christ and the Christian life, please write us without obligation: Moody Press, c/o MLM, Chicago, Illinois 60610.